Priya Doty

FINDING WARRIOR POSE

FINDING WARRIOR POSE

PRIYA DOTY

NEW YORK

This book was inspired by the joy of traveling.
When one is completely lost in their surroundings,
they are immersed in the present.

PRIYA DOTY

FINDING WARRIOR POSE

CHAPTER ONE

Holi Hai

When Holi is occurring, those celebrating it say "Holi Hai", which means: Holi simply is, right here, all around us, unavoidable, everywhere you turn, a flash mob of a good time that rolls everyone up in its wake, no matter how strenuously they try to avoid it. Holi is the Indian festival of spring, and it is celebrated with bright colors and harmless mischief and, for some, raucous partying. For Jaya, the first Holi celebration of the year happened on a cloudy Saturday afternoon, when the Central New Jersey Indian Association threw its annual Happy Holi Youth & Family Mixer. She was feeling vaguely annoyed that she had to be there at all. Her family had guilted her into coming instead of staying in New York City, where she lived. And she was also angry at herself, for not having the courage to go on a casual coffee hang with a guy she'd met online. Instead of answering his messages, she had created vivid rituals in her mind of *when* she would respond to him (i.e., after she spackled that hole in her wall, returned her aunt's phone calls, and mastered bread making). There was always something better to do, it seemed. And so, now, as she stood at the entrance of the Holi party, wondering why her life choices had put her here instead of on a date—any date—she was feeling a distinct lack of accomplishment. As a single woman, she often felt that she was waiting for her life to begin. That, of course, would be when she was considered to be a "real person" by her family and their friends, someone with a "real place to live", in a "real city". The problem was that Jaya didn't know what would convince her family. Was it a relationship, a job, a new place, a trip? That unsettled, anxious feeling seemed to be stalking her more frequently as she entered her thirties, telling her she'd better get on with it and start her life, before it was too late. When change did come knocking, as she was to find out in the ensuing months, it appeared suddenly. It turns out there are certain events and times, and people and places, that on occasion defy the natural order of things. That, despite the social patterns encoded into the behavior of the human race, exceptions continue to exist. Ultimately, she was to learn that reality has its own pathways, punctuated with aha moments, small successes, joys, and failures. Seemingly short episodes come to define longer arcs of time. This certainly was the case for Jaya. Jaya Gupta, actually, if names are being recorded.

This year, the Happy Holi Youth & Family Mixer was thankfully being held indoors. This was in response to the large volume of complaints received last year, when the outdoor location and a mid-March slush storm caused everyone to tiptoe around in their chappal sandals as they valiantly threw colored powders at one another, ignoring the cold rising up their toes. This year's committee made the wise and gracious choice to shift the celebration into a Greek-owned indoor wedding hall. That said, effective logistical planning was not frequently of concern to Association members. Truly, they reveled in disorganized events, with late starts, delayed catering, and last-minute program changes a common occurrence. In another surprise, the normally thrifty attendees forked over $50 a head to be kept intact and dry, ignoring the steep rise from last year's $5 entry fee. A few months from now, they would grumble about this, too, when the cost of cleaning the carpets stained with colored powders would lead to an unforeseen $11,000 charge that the Association again would have to bear. And the pendulum would then swing back to hosting the event outside in a large empty parking lot, where participants the following year would be admonished to wear snow boots.

Despite the poor planning, the Association's members dutifully attended each year's celebrations. They couldn't imagine any other way. Chaotic logistics and creature discomforts, after all, simply reminded them of home. It was normal and good, and perhaps a bit okay, to tolerate disorder amid American softness.

At midday, thin light from the chandeliers shone dully over all as a particulate mess of colors, emulsified in water and drifting above in a haze, after being shot through water guns, water semi-automatic rifles, and water crocodiles. And below? People in old, ratty sweatpants and saris that would soon be turned into rags winced as they tried to avoid eye contact with the water color war taking place. Teenage girls boldly smeared globs of green powder on the too-cool high school boy (so sweet!) who had broken all stereotypes but somehow managed to wear a varsity football jacket. Five-year-olds screeched with joy as they ran from dads chasing them monster-like, hands curled over their heads and backs hunched as they followed the little boys around the room. Grandpas stood in a corner, staring silently at the carpet and bonding over tacit, manly things. The post-college singles drew together in a pack by the cool-drinks table, recreating the bars they went to on the weekends. Cliques formed organically based on profession, based on original Indian language, based on who shopped on sale and who always paid full price. Grandmas rested their aching, sandaled heels on cafeteria chairs with faux leather padding. Which is where Jaya found herself sitting, slightly apart and hovering like a satellite, among a tight group consisting of Daadi Ma and her friends: three grandmas wearing identical coke-bottle glasses, their hair in buns, and knitted cardigans tastefully covering their midsections. Next to them was a large-for-his-age grandchild of fourteen, who was too self-assuredly nerdy to play with the rest, named Vivek. It was Vivek who spoke out of turn, as per usual.

"Is it true you are going to a yoga ashram for six months?" he asked, directing the question at Jaya, without stating her name, which would be disrespectful.

Jaya shifted her slim frame in the banquet hall chair, instinctively pulling on a lock of her long, thick black hair as a defense mechanism.

"Yes!" Daadi Ma replied, forcefully, pumping a turquoise-stained fist into the air. "She go! To my village!"

"Wait, Daadi Ma! You told people? I didn't agree to anything yet," Jaya interrupted, her green eyes flashing. But it was too late. The topic of conversation set, Jaya's grandmother and her friends leaned in to discuss, salty snacks within reach.

"Wah, wah, Jaya, this is pfhan-tastic!" said the loud grandma, Mrs. Patel, in the purple sari.

"So brave! Smaaart girl!" said Mrs. Agarwala, the sweet grandma in a pink salwar kameez.

"You will love it! My granddaughter does won-derful yoga," Mrs. Malhotra, the pushy grandma in a yellow blouse, added knowingly.

"Isn't it loud in India? How will you be able to do yoga there?" Vivek inquired in a non sequitur.

"Silly boy," Mrs. Patel said to Vivek, "don't you know yoga was started in India, so they have a way."

"But, okay, to be clear," Jaya said emphatically, giving Daadi Ma an exasperated look. "I haven't decided to definitely go yet."

"Well, Sharmila," Mrs. Patel said to Daadi Ma, "surely you will convince her to go. This is for her own good."

"Yes, yes, all arrangements have been made. She go for six months, for free!" Daadi Ma said excitedly, nodding her head in such a way as to insist that it was final. She sniffed afterwards, for good measure, a sort of punctuation that indicated the discussion was closed.

Jaya was still a bit groggy from waking up so early to get here from the city, so she didn't have the energy to stop the train of conversation that was barreling through now. As she listened dispassionately about her future being laid out for her, she tried to remember how this had all started anyway.

Oh right, she thought, *the land record*. Daadi Ma had sprung the news last weekend. Her father's family had once owned a piece of land in his hometown, Maalpur, situated in the absolute center of India, in Madhya Pradesh, which translates into "middle state". This small town was apparently, Daadi Ma had said, now the site of a well-known yoga ashram. At the time, Jaya hadn't understood why the ashram was so important to her family. But then again, at the time, she was a mess.

Last Saturday, Jaya, having nothing better to do, grudgingly agreed to meet her parents and grandmother at their house in New Jersey. Her drive was easy, devoid of traffic and aggressive drivers, which gave her lots of time to zone out and think. Looking on the positive side, she wondered if perhaps seeing her family would help her feel better about the whole job situation.

The day before, at 3 pm, Jaya had been called into her boss's office and told her role as an IT project manager was being eliminated.

"Out of my control, you see," her boss, Steve, had said apologetically. The thirtysomething manager, who was not much older than herself, was quick to point out that the edict to let people go had "come down from upper management" when they had decided to cancel the entire new billing system project that Jaya was working on. Of course, he explained, the laid-off staff would get two months' severance and during that time, the opportunity to apply for other positions at the insurance company, which, he assured Jaya, would be an option for her.

"Really, Jaya, you're a hard worker and smart, and I wouldn't worry if I were you. You'll stay on our payroll for another two months, and I'm confident we'll find you something else to work on at this company, or you'll find a better job somewhere else, and this will all blow over. You're young and single, with no responsibilities to a family. You've got nothing to worry about."

Shell-shocked by this turn of events, Jaya didn't press Steve too much, other than to ask a few pertinent questions about her benefits, and when the rest of the team would know. Back at her gray cubicle, she composed a goodbye note to her teammates, threw a few key things into her large day bag, and dumped the rest of the contents of her desk into a cardboard box marked for recycling. She was pretty sure she would not need to return on Monday. Or if she wanted to.

On her way home, the city beckoned her. As always, the city on a Friday was full of mystery. You could walk through all sorts of neighborhoods—rich, staid, wild, touristy—seemingly traipsing through worlds separated by only a block or two. There were streets dedicated to wholesale florists, others to only Brazilian restaurants; some sections were taken over by the craft services trucks of movie shoots; and riverfront avenues were bombarded with athletic runners. Now, she wandered aimlessly, skipping the subway, walking through random neighborhoods on her way back to her Murray Hill apartment, stopping for beers along the way. It was a good distraction to throw herself into other people's worlds for the afternoon while she felt so rudderless and confused. The day's events were followed by a terrible date with a guy she shouldn't have given another chance to. The date with David had ended with her storming out of the bar after he accused her of dating him for his money. As if.

But today was Saturday, and she was feeling virtuous for going to see her family, which lifted her mood just the tiniest bit. She arrived at her parents' house, fitting her midsize Japanese sedan into the narrow driveway that was barely wide enough for one car. The feeling of being dissatisfied with everything, from her dating life, to her work life, to her general existence, pulsed through her like fear as she flopped out of her car. Surely, there was something to hold onto? But she wasn't sure what.

"If I'm lucky," she said to herself, "if I'm lucky, they won't ask me about marriage today. I just couldn't take it. Not this week. Not after last night. Just this once, please."

The pressure to "settle down" had definitely been ratcheting up. It didn't make any sense, really, to Jaya. How was she supposed to find someone to marry just like that, because she had reached the appropriate age? Not to mention, did her parents and her grandmother even understand what dating in New York was like? It was impossible to get a second date these days, let alone a third, or something approaching a relationship that might lead to marriage. And yet, Daadi Ma pressed on. Jaya recalled a conversation with her recently. Daadi Ma, barely five feet tall, wearing socks and flip-flops, a loose sari and her trademark cardigan, her hair in a bun, her glasses slipping down her tiny nose, had spoken much too loudly in her imperfect immigrant's English. It was a unidirectional monologue, peppered with grammatical innovations, stream of consciousness, and general hyperbole. One of Daadi Ma's best, on a topic that might have been entitled "In which the elders find a suitable groom for their daughter".

"My granddaughter darling child, daughter of my firstborn son," she had said, "Time is now. You don't... wait... too long. Do not be like Mrs. Singh's son. You know, he is forty-six and unmarried, balding, heavyset. What young lady will they find for him now? And her daughter, tsch! Forty-one years old, wearing short short skirts and not yet married and dating these fast boys. Our traditions are for many reasons. You, Jaya, are smart girl and trust your Daadi Ma. You will find boy, settle down, then find love. You will find. But you must not waste time anymore. So beautiful, you are just like film star Parvis. Beautiful, she died in fire, dark long hair. Green eyes! Different. You will find, good, sober boy."

"Insane," her roommate MJ had said when Jaya had relayed this story to her over the finest boxed wine they could find. Ten years into their great experiment of living in this fine city, Jaya and MJ considered themselves "official" New Yorkers. They had met their freshman year at a liberal arts college in the northeast, moved to the city after graduating, and had never looked back. "Verifiably insane," her pale, red-headed friend had continued. "Did she pull that stuff again, about honoring your family's traditions? She has got to stop with that, it's messing with your mind. It's a lot of guilt, you know?"

As Jaya walked up to her parents' house, she could smell the familiar aroma of an onion-and-tomato-based dish cooking. The door was unlocked, as always. Food could be a cure and a salve when emotions were too complicated. This certainly seemed to be the modus operandi for Daadi Ma, her mom, and likely all of her female relatives before them. Then again, there wasn't anything wrong with this, Jaya thought, as she heard her mom's voice from the kitchen.

"Jaya! Come just now and help me pour this in the strainer. It's heavy, and I need to get the water out," she called. Her mom, Kiran, was what they called a live wire in the Indian community in this part of New Jersey. She was short, plump, and frequently multicolored. Today she was wearing a magenta top and matching capri pants, high-heeled magenta sandals, big dangly earrings, blue eyeliner that curled up at the corners of her eyes, and hot pink lipstick. Her frizzy hair was held back on one side with a comb affixed with magenta-hued crystals that did not occur in nature. Her nails were painted a similar pink, slightly too long and looking out of place on her rather fleshy fingers.

"Coming!" Jaya said as she quickly slipped off her shoes and deposited them on a small rug that sat next to the front door for this purpose.

The house was a visual feast with every square inch of vertical space covered with photographs and wall hangings. Furniture sat among Ganesh statues, decorated mirrors with carved wooden frames, and fancy throw textiles with elephants on them. To Jaya, it was simply home. Even her room upstairs was the same as she'd left it when she had moved out.

"There you are," Daadi Ma said as Jaya walked into the kitchen. "Your mother is making roti and fresh food." Daadi Ma sat cross-legged in a large lounge chair just outside the open kitchen, holding court, with her feet tucked under her loose, light purple sari. Kiran's arms were sunk deep into a ball of flour, and her bright gold bangles were pushed back almost to her elbows.

As usual, Jaya's father was on a high barstool, his arms propped on the marble-topped island in the middle of the kitchen, fixated on his tablet and scrolling through his work emails. Nitin, who normally went by NT so that his engineering colleagues could pronounce his name properly, was a focused man dedicated to his career, and he left the running of the house to his mother, who in turn outsourced much of the daily activities to her daughter-in-law.

Daadi Ma exuded a warmth and good-heartedness that Jaya craved, and she went over and hugged her, plopping down on a seat next to her.

"Haan, yes! Eat! Find boy! Settle down," Daadi Ma said, as usual, obsessed with the marriage thing. Apparently, Jaya would not be left alone this day.

"Hi, Daadi Ma," Jaya said as she kissed her cheek. "I'm actually trying to lose weight."

"He! Lose weight. What is this? Mother-in-laws like healthy women. You eat! You..." Daadi Ma held out her hands, showing her confusion that anyone would desire to be skinny. Her exhortation was cut off by a breaking news alert on her satellite TV, where an Indian channel was reporting the untimely death of a film star who had been popular in the 1950s. "Tsch. So sad. Go with God. She the one, Jaya, I say who looks like you!"

Jaya rolled her eyes. Daadi Ma was nothing if not consistent, in that she was able to carry on a running commentary on just about anything.

"Ma!" Kiran said. "Show Jaya what you were wanting to show her. Food will be ready shortly. Why not go get it, while we are finishing the bread?"

The kitchen was a place of constant experimentation. Glass jars of spices sat on the shelves, frequently refilled by larger plastic bags of the same spices that were stored in the pantry. With the liberal amount of spices that Kiran added to most of her dishes, refills were frequently required.

Mother and daughter stood side by side. Jaya, without asking, had taken her usual post. She grabbed a handful of premade dough, rolled the dough in flour, flattened it with her hand, powdered it again with flour, and then pushed the rolling pin through it. When she was done, she handed the finished product to her mother, who gently slipped it into a dark brown–black wok filled with boiling oil.

The roti-making continued as Daadi Ma got up. Jaya rolled her eyes internally, hoping she wasn't about to be shown someone's dating profile, or as it was called in the Indian community, biodata. She'd already been through this, with the son of her father's classmate; he had turned out to be an uninteresting, arrogant anesthesiologist with an interest in marriage and children, and a total lack of interest in who would fill that role. Jaya shuddered, thinking of the date at the Chinese chain restaurant and how awkward it had been. She tensed, preparing herself for battle, for whatever Daadi Ma was planning.

"Child. You come here. Have something," Daadi Ma said.

"Okay? Like what?" Jaya was in the midst of fixing up another round of rotis.

"Come, come here!" Daadi Ma insisted, vigorously nodding as if to will Jaya to move, while beckoning with one outstretched hand to signal Jaya to come closer.

"I can't, hands are floured." Jaya raised her hands to show Daadi Ma.

"Oof, okay. I come there." Daadi Ma got up and walked over. "Here, see this. What I found." She held up a flimsy piece of paper so Jaya could read it while she worked on the rotis.

"What is it?" Jaya asked.

"Property deed!" her father piped up, momentarily looking up from his emails.

Daadi Ma waved the thin foreign-looking paper with its chicken scratchings and slapped it once for good measure.

"From MY grandfather. We own. Big big land. Now an ashram. Yoga place. Fancy! American and European people go. You will go."

The paper wilted in the air, refusing to stand upright of its own volition during Daadi Ma's speech. That's how Jaya knew it was from the old country. The hardy evergreens of the Pacific Northwest produced a different sort of paper.

"Um, huh? We own property in India? No one ever told me about this," Jaya said, confused.

"Remember what we talked about," Kiran said, ominously looking toward Daadi Ma. "You must give her time to make her decision."

"My decision? What?!" Jaya inwardly groaned at this new scheme from her grandmother. Surely it involved some type of romantic setup or even worse, an arranged marriage. "What is wrong with you guys? Can't I do my laundry and eat in peace?" Jaya felt the dissatisfaction of the past few days seep in. The sore spots from losing her role at work, the weirdness of the date with David, and the fear of zero dating prospects in the months ahead.

"Tsch. Listen, Jaya. Your grandmother"—here her mother looked sternly at Daadi Ma, who was doing her best to appear nonchalant while quietly sitting and sipping her tea—"your grandmother and your father and I think that you would benefit from seeing some of your history, our family history."

"You go to India. See tradition. Land is gone, you see. Gone! This, just for you to see, look, meet guru, do yoga, be in our tradition. Then you come back, find boy, then settle. Maybe love," Daadi Ma said, sniffing. She crossed her arms as if to say she wouldn't change her position on this subject.

"Okay, you guys are nuts." At this Jaya grabbed a freshly cooked roti off the griddle, began to pat butter on it, then thought better of it and started picking off pieces to munch. It was hot where pockets of air seeped out, and she blew on the roti to cool it.

"Really, Jaya, we are not as you say 'nuts'," her father said. "We just think this will be good for you—you're young! You should get out and explore the world! And we have this property, that the yoga ashram people stole from us, so why shouldn't you bloody go stay there. All you have to do is go to India, and then they will take care of the rest!"

Jaya contemplated what her father said, and what there was for her here—she had no boys, no responsibilities, no job. And her future seemed about as unknowable as an empty road leading into a stark wilderness in the middle of a foggy night. She thought about what MJ would do in this situation—*Take it, surely*—then immediately dismissed this whole thing as crazy.

"Okay, you guys, seriously I just wanted a chill afternoon. I need to get a job. Pay my bills. Responsibilities. I can't believe I'm saying this to you—yes, I'm the one talking responsibilities now—but it's just that... I don't think, I mean, I'll think about it, okay? Now can we please eat?" Jaya had no intention whatsoever of thinking about this and planned to forget about it at her first opportunity, which would be on her drive home, escaping from this impossible imposition.

Back at the banquet hall, Daadi Ma held her audience in rapt attention.

"Before," she began, throwing her hand back with her statement and lightly tilting her head. "My grandfather. He have big land. In Maalpur. Near railway station."

The grandmas nodded knowingly. They had all at one time or the other been through Maalpur's train station, before the railways transferred from British to Indian control, before World War II and Indian independence.

"It our land," Daadi Ma continued, "meaning grandfather's land, my grandfather," here she looked at Jaya, "your GREAT-GREAT-grandfather. As is custom, you see? The land was divided to give equal share to each of the sons, so my father, Jaya, your GREAT-grandfather, he receive one out of NINE parts of the land. You follow? The land is good, but where to find work? One by one the brothers left to big city. The village has no electricity, no lights, no water. Why stay there? One brother, he die very young. Cholera. Only one brother, Prasanjit, he was only brother of my father, he stay."

"But, sister, if YOUR land is sitting in Maalpur, then how are you here in New Jersey?" asked Mrs. Agarwala, the sweet one dressed in pink.

"Eh, people stole it, I think. No?" interjected Mrs. Malhotra, the pushy one in yellow.

"Pardon, but I thought Indian people did not steal because it is not correct?" Vivek asked.

"Oh, Vivek, you are such as SIMPLE boy," said Jaya, mimicking a thick Indian accent. Vivek shrugged and looked at his phone.

"What to do? Prasanjit Uncle, he had son, Pupinder. That son he good friends with the local police inspector. He wait, wait until alllll the grandfather's sons have left to big city and then he say the WHOLE land is his and bribe his police friends and he take the land. It was bad situation. Then, suddenly, he die. Bus accident. Quite common. Then, nothing heard. Then suddenly yoga ashram is there. My son, your father Jaya, he try, long time back, to get land, police, courts, he try try try, but it is too late now. It is gone. New Jersey is our home now. We are happy," Daadi Ma finished.

"This is all bribes," Mrs. Malhotra said definitively.

"One HUNDRED percent bribery and thievery," said Mrs. Patel, flicking her hand to stress the totality of it and shutting her eyes for emphasis.

"But, ladies, I am thinking that at least Jaya will see her home village, you know?" said Mrs. Agarwala, always looking on the bright side. She smiled as she spoke.

"Exactly!" said Daadi Ma, throwing a pointed finger in the air. She had the triumphant expression of someone solving a difficult math problem, displaying her brilliance as she casually wrote out a proof on a chalkboard while all these simpletons around her gaped in awe. Daadi Ma waited for the others to catch on.

"But if the land is gone, how did you come to..." Jaya started.

"Social media! Of course!" Daadi Ma declared. "I find on the online the yoga ashram in Maalpur, peh, so much fakery. Fake guruji and made-up nonsense to make money from foreign peoples. I call, I say, 'I am from Maalpur, this my land' and we have instant message talk and then they invite us to come!"

"And you didn't lay any guilt on them? You know, for owning the land that was technically yours? They just thought to invite us? Just like that?" Jaya asked, becoming suspicious almost by instinct, voicing her thoughts in front of the aunties despite herself. Daadi Ma was stubborn and determined. She must have badgered these people into helping her.

"Me? Guilt?" Daadi Ma looked up, her eyes large in the magnified lenses, speaking in a tone of exaggerated innocence. Turning to her friends, she said, "Now, Jaya will take big trip to India. Six months! To ashram!" She raised her hand to her granddaughter's taller frame and patted her shoulder awkwardly, hunching forward at the same time.

Jaya frowned. "But Daadi Ma, I haven't agreed to anything yet! I thought we'd talk about this later?"

Vivek looked up from his phone, in awe of this real-time display of elder disrespect. His own grandmother would never have brooked this level of back talk in his home. He clutched his device tighter, remembering the last time his phone privileges had been taken away.

"Six MONTHS!" Jaya continued, with more vehemence. "How am I supposed to go six months without work? I only got two months' severance and I have to make rent!" As she spoke, she realized she was belying what she felt inside, which was hope, a bit of a spark and a bit of curiosity. But taking time off seemed impossible, irresponsible. And Jaya always felt she was practical, predictable, dependable, boring even. Her colleagues viewed her as a rock whom they could rely on to keep them on deadline, even when their plans didn't always go as expected. She'd worked her whole life to have the right job and be a productive person, and this idea of leaving on a six-month hiatus seemed frivolous and unlike her.

"Six months?" her mom said, interrupting Jaya's thoughts as she approached with a tray of fresh samosas, which Mrs. Malhotra promptly and eagerly reached for. The food had only just arrived from the caterers; it was two hours late, which meant the time for hors d'oeuvres had been pushed back. "Oooh, I like them hot," Mrs. Malhotra whispered, a bit self-consciously.

"Jaya, honey, can't you treat it like a sabbatical?" Kiran continued. "They do it all the time on the TV—young women and men take time off so they can go travel the world and live like sadhus and go find themselves. Everyone's doing it, Jaya." She spoke with an air of sophistication as she waved her hand in the air, sending a scent of perfume Jaya's way. "Really, it's the modern way."

Mrs. Agarwala was nodding, and the other grandmas quickly followed her cue. Kiran was dropping some deep wisdom now, which the grandmothers approved of.

"A sabbatical? What?" Jaya said with a quiver to her voice. "You want me to leave New York and my apartment so I can randomly go to India for six months? All because Daadi Ma found the deed to some property that is now a yoga ashram that no one knew about until now?"

"Jaya, what are you so worried about? Jobs come and go. You'll find another one, and your dad and I can cover you if you need money," Kiran said.

"You must try," Daadi Ma said, fuming. She did not like to be crossed. Especially not in front of her friends, who all believed that she ruled her house with an iron fist.

"Pah, this yoga ashram in the middle of Maalpur? Sharmila, really? Jaya will be TOH-tally bored. She's a city girl!" Mrs. Malhotra said, trying to lighten the mood. "She needs to see the fun things. Do you want to do a weekend trip to Mumbai, sweetie? I have my sister's daughter there, and she can take you around."

"And, sweetheart, but do you speak Hindi? How will you get around? That area in Maalpur is not very touristy or modern. You will find most will be more comfortable speaking Hindi with you," said Mrs. Agarwala.

"She have no problem with Hindi!" Daadi Ma declared defiantly, turning to Jaya and seemingly daring her to begin speaking in Hindi on command. But Jaya wasn't completely paying attention.

Absurd. That's what Jaya was thinking. *This idea was absurd.* What she rejected about this trip, she reflected, was that it felt so illogical and unplanned, that the reason to go seemed to come abruptly out of nowhere. This approach to life was a source of tension between her rational, mostly Western-trained mind, and her mom and grandma, who delighted in the emotional, circular Eastern logic in which they had been raised. To them, the *why* was never important; instead, they focused entirely on reacting to the *here* and *now*. Beyond that, though, she had to admit her mom was right about something. Her job search could wait. She could take some time off, come back in six months, and find something then. Her parents would support her if she needed cash. And India couldn't be that expensive. It was possible. She'd surely like to see India, even though it might be weird and big and scary to go without her family.

And hell, it wasn't as if she had some big boyfriend or love life to keep up at home.

She thought back to her last conversation with her mother. They had been standing in the kitchen at home, side by side.

Her mom had said, "You've worked so hard to get good grades, get through college, and you've established yourself after college and then you got a great job, and yes, you'll find another one, and you're living in New York City all by yourself and still you are such a good girl. But you've never been to your father's hometown and now the land is gone anyway. This is the last connection, honey, that your Daadi Ma has created for you. So, honor this past of yours. You will be thankful. Six months is nothing."

Jaya came out of her reverie when Mrs. Malhotra of the yellow blouse touched her arm. "If anyone touches you like this! See, what I'm doing? You push them away. Fast. Possible for leprosy, you know. Many people still have leprosy."

Not to be outdone with shocking yet banal advice, Mrs. Patel of the purple sari interjected, "Do not trust homemade street foods at all. Best to order food that is hot and cooked in a clean environment. Especially not the train station stalls. Could be anything. One time, I even pulled out a frog. They made pickle out of it. Can you believe it?" She clutched her stomach for effect.

"But sweetheart, will you be looking for marriage prospects when you are there? Oh Sharmila, she must. In fact, my very own sister-in-law just sent her son there for marriage, and he came back with a wonderful bride," said Mrs. Agarwala of the pink salwar kameez, clapping her hands in glee.

Jaya stood up, aiming to gain some control of the conversation. "I hate to disappoint you all, but I'm not sure this is quite the adventure you think it is. It's a yoga ashram, you know? Wake up every day at 5 am and eat only plain rice and lentils and yogurt, I'm sure. It's going to be pretty boring. Where would I even see someone with leprosy? Or selling frogs made into pickles? You must be pulling my leg!"

"In train station," Daadi Ma sniffed, "train from Delhi to Maalpur."

"It's true," echoed Mrs. Malhotra. "In these train stations, you can find most anything undesirable. It is a hot spot of bad behavior and pestilence."

Jaya sighed. "Let's hope not," she said, unconvincingly.

CHAPTER TWO

Yoga 101

The festivities continued the next day at Holi Hang-eroverama, a color party out toward the East River in Williamsburg, Brooklyn. The event's name was a play on words, Jaya explained as she, MJ and MJ's boyfriend, Mark, entered the large outdoor lot, got their hands stamped, and paid the entrance fee. "Because 'hungama' is a Hindi word that means like, a party, a 'Hangoverama' on a Sunday afternoon is a party for nursing Saturday's hangover."

"I like the color aspect," Mark said, somewhat daintily for such a burly guy. "It's cool that you get to play with colors and stuff, and it's just fun and a good time. I mean, you don't think it's like, weird or anything that we're celebrating your holiday, do you, Jaya?"

She laughed. "No, it's cool. I like that people even care enough to 'culturally appropriate' us," she joked, saying the words while pantomiming air quotes. As far as she was concerned, she was thrilled that other people wanted to celebrate her culture. It made it more fun and interesting, if others liked it, too. Her thoughts were interrupted by a slender man approaching them now. He looked to be about twenty-five with light brown hair cut short on the sides and longish on top.

"MJ!"

"Kevin!"

"HELLO!" they both screamed. Kisses were exchanged.

Kevin used to work with MJ at her hip Union Square office, where she was a quality manager for an online jewelry shopping website. He was now a party promoter. When he spoke, as he did now, he bent—forward to hear MJ's response and backwards to laugh and sideways when he got going on a subject. He was wearing a 90s-era flannel shirt in red—it was open all the way showing a plain white T-shirt underneath—tan khaki shorts despite the wintry weather, and rough-looking black work boots. There were words rushing out of Kevin as he got out a number of very important things that he'd apparently wanted to tell MJ all at once, over the three minutes he would talk to her, until he saw her again in six months, somewhere out and about, when they would talk for another three minutes. Jaya hated this about New York: how it could sometimes be such a vacuous place. There were so many millions of people here, but it was quantity over quality. Meaningful friendships shouldn't be built on short intervals over an elapsed time of one year. Right now, Kevin was doing his best to fill up his three minutes, while Jaya smiled at the appropriate times and rolled her eyes.

"...Great scene this is SO fun we MUST get together and there are just SO many people and this year the event is just becoming SO SO popular and oh hey, who are your friends? Is this your boyfriend? Oh HI Mark, I've heard SO much about you! And Jaya, hi Jaya, are you SO impressed with our little Holi celebration? I mean, don't you just LOVE bhangra because I was at this all-night thing last night, an all-night bhangra rave and it was SO awesome and there were the BEST-looking people there but anyway MJ SERIOUSLY we MUST get together. I'll be back!" And he was off.

The scene that Kevin left them in was a public school's athletic playground lot. Under an overcast sky, tents had been set up on a light-green racetrack to sell food and dispense beer and colored powder; bleachers of light aluminum sat on the sides; and everything was bordered by a low-lying chain-link fence. Incongruously, there was a basketball hoop off to the left side, with the net still on it, a sure sign that it was well cared for and probably locked down during off-hours. Crushed in the middle of the lot were crowds of people, all young or younger than Jaya's group, wearing ratty sweatpants and short shorts and long boots and bandannas and sweaters. Everyone was smeared in various colors of powder, laughing, shout-talking, dancing, and holding dripping beers in overfilled plastic cups as they walked unsteadily through packs of people. A girl was sitting off to the side smoking a clove cigarette while making balloon animals and handing them to random passersby. Wordlessly, she held out a balloon hot dog to Mark, who took it with a slight bow, as they walked by.

"This is rad," MJ pronounced. She and Mark were soon in the crowd, jumping up and down to the music while holding each other's arms. They were two of a kind—heavyset but limber, tossing their hair and dancing their cares away. Mark had blue powder smeared throughout his dark, curly hair, and MJ's green face accentuated her red hair. Both were smiling like loons.

Moving from spot to spot and attempting to look like she belonged, despite her singlehood, Jaya circled the vendor stands to avoid going into the throng of people. There was no meaning in this, Jaya thought as she halfheartedly perused a stall selling burritos stuffed with cilantro-infused pork, nor tradition. People were here, throwing themselves about, not because they understood Holi to be a rite of spring. They were here not because they were expected to show up at the annual event put on by the Indian association. They were here, she realized as she grabbed a sample of chocolate-covered cumin seeds from another vendor, for novelty. For something different on a random boring Sunday in March, she thought as she crunched the strangely tangy chocolate, and because they were tired of winter and this had colors and it might be fun. As she rounded on another stall filled with pamphlets and staffed by a smiling man in a turban, she came full circle. After all, she thought as she picked up a pamphlet showing people in body-bending stretches, wasn't the purpose of Holi to celebrate spring and the end of winter? Weren't they doing just that? And more to the point, sure, the American youth weren't farmers waiting for a harvest as her ancestors did in pastoral societies, but didn't spring bring much in the way of possibility? New trips, new loves, new clothes. It could count, couldn't it? She looked up and smiled back at the smiling man.

"What are you thinking about?" asked the man, who looked about forty but still youthful, the only giveaway being the slight gray strands of hair that peaked out of his turban near his ears. Those and his choice of pants, which were pulled up a little high over a slight middle-aged spread. "It's just, you look so serious."

"Oh, me? Oh, I was spacing out, I guess," Jaya said.

"You must honor your mental space, always. Namaste," the man replied with his palms held together. "Well, we are here today with the K.J. Yoga Studio, where we have three options for beginners and two options for intermediate students. And if you're an advanced yogi, then we can set up private lessons. We have a special right now—one month completely free when you sign up for three months. That's... a thirty-three percent discount." The last bit, the one with the percentage, he said with a slight frown, as if the realpolitik of selling and of calculations about the value of things was highly distasteful.

"Oh, I um, well, I don't think I'm interested," she started, almost out of habit as a standard response to someone asking her to buy something. But then she remembered the yoga ashram and thought maybe this was a sign. Maybe she was coming around to Daadi Ma's idea. After all, how bad could it be, really?

Words she didn't expect rushed out of her now. "Well actually, I might need to learn yoga. I guess I'm a beginner. But, oh, I don't have three months. Could you do one month?"

"For sure, the introductory thing, that's for the people who need packages, you know? Some people need more structure, but if you are more willing to free-flow it, then it's just twenty-four dollars a class, and that's absolutely right on, too. I'm Gary by the way."

Jaya found herself going along with Gary without much pushback, just to grab a piece of his calm kindness. She filled out her details for a class later in the week and forked over payment, even telling him to keep the change. She did need to reclaim her mental space. He was right about that. She felt at home nowhere. There was no structure to her life, no office to go to, no reason to get up in the morning. An uncertain future lay ahead involving self-indulgent idleness and who knew what. Amongst the hipsters joyously celebrating a holiday of her heritage, she felt like a sort of spinster curmudgeon, unable to let go and have a good time while everyone around her was letting loose. Amongst the gossip grandmas of New Jersey, she felt like an oddity, a pampered only daughter being encouraged to take an unwise detour from an otherwise respectable life, whilst their grandchildren got married and had kids, went to grad schools, and became doctors and lawyers. Perhaps, she thought, she might at least be able to hold onto this one thing, until she arrived at the next solid thing in her life, whenever that might be—and with the hope that it, too, wouldn't leave her behind.

Things soon fell into place. Jaya found herself calling her ex-boss, Steve, gracefully telling him that no, she would not be looking for a new role at the insurance company, and promising to send pictures of her yoga adventure so that he and her old colleagues could live vicariously through her. She even laughed while she did it. MJ's boyfriend agreed to take Jaya's portion of the rent and move into their apartment while she was in India. It was a prelude to MJ and Mark living together permanently, and though Jaya knew that this meant her time as MJ's roommate was likely coming to an end, she resolved not to think about it until she returned. Right now, she couldn't handle any more change. With all of the logistics to arrange and tasks to finish before leaving, Jaya built a project management spreadsheet for her life, instead of for her job. Today's entry was typical:

Column 1: Moving. Today's Row: Decide which books to keep, pack books in a box. Put box in car. Put books to be given away in main hallway.

Column 2: Learning Yoga. Today's Row: Yoga class @ 4pm

Her first yoga class was a revelation. To get there, Jaya took the subway to an industrial area surrounding 30th Street and the West Side Highway. She buzzed a green-gray metal door and waited to be let inside, wondering why the studio had to be in such an unattractive place. Gary could be heard from the bottom of the stairwell, and as Jaya walked up the steps—taller than normal steps, hard metal, requiring some careful navigation—his voice became louder and louder.

"Ma. Ma! Ma, you aren't listening to me. You put the phone in the charger at night. Then, the alarm rings. The alarms—remember, Ma—the alarms remind you to take your medications. Ma, no, I'm not yelling at you. I just want to be very clear that you need to... okay... okay.... Get the nurse on the phone."

He was still wearing that turban from the Hangoverama party and a purple T-shirt with holes peeking out of the waist area. He was thin of arm and leg but chunky at the stomach and hips, of medium height. His arms were covered in darkish brown hair and tattoos. His demeanor changed when she approached. Now he was all calm and collected, the trials of an aging mother forgotten as he focused on the job at hand. As he oriented her on where she could change, get a mat and so forth, the buzzer rang a dozen more times, and the hollow noise of her classmates making the journey up the stairs filled the room. Yoga mats swished against the wooden floorboards, their users positioning themselves in their favorite spots. Jaya sat where she felt comfortable: in the back of the room, awaiting further instructions while eyeing jealously the women who seemed to be perfectly thin, wearing the right brand of yoga pants. She told herself that she went to the gym, to classes like Super Barre and Step 95 and The Dance Method, and that she could do intervals and weights for at least forty-five minutes at a time; whatever this was, it couldn't possibly be a challenge.

That opinion was to be sorely tested as soon as they started. It wasn't long before a copious amount of sweat was rolling down her light brown shoulders and dripping onto the increasingly slick rental yoga mat. Her hair was all wet, and not just at the top of her head but underneath, too, at her neck. The sweat streaked down her arms in little rivulets. It pooled between her toes. She even felt trickles running down her back to meet the waistband of her running shorts. Around her, the serene women were completely cool and dry, with mildly beatific looks on their faces as they calmly held impossible poses for minutes on end. As if they weren't so much in an exercise class, but saints and nuns pardoning the weak and the hungry. Now Gary told them to hold something called the warrior pose, and Jaya's thighs burned, her raised arms started to shake, and she cursed the chaturanga push-ups she'd just done and wondered why she'd thought yoga was easy. Perhaps, she thought as she gritted her teeth while holding her pose for another ten seconds, perhaps only the yoga that Daadi Ma watched on Indian TV was easy. She recalled women in salwar kameez stretching and rolling their wrists and ankles. This, however, this was something altogether different. If morning TV yoga for seventy-year-olds was a light stroll, this was a half-marathon.

Salvation came at last in the form of the floor, forty-five minutes in, when Gary indicated they should get comfortable in something called savasana. Jaya watched as her fellow classmates rushed to the front of the class to pick up Mexican-style blankets, so she did the same. Gary switched off the lights and played music that was full of gongs and bells, and told everyone to lie down and relax. With her body exhausted, Jaya did exactly that. She felt permission to let her mind go. She experienced the sensation of small shapes of colors dancing in front of her eyes. In the silence, a courage rose and she envisioned the pains of the recent past. The scene in her boss's office when her job had been eliminated, and his surprise that she wouldn't stick around to stay for another role. Her grandmother, egging her on to go to India. The second date with David and what a disaster it had been. She winced, remembering how he had confused her with someone else, asking her about her trip to Istanbul. When she'd confronted him about this, he dug in, insisting that she (and all other women) were the same, because they wanted to use finance guys like him for the cash flow. Well, that did it. There was something so deeply, and obviously, offensive about this that Jaya had gotten up, thrown some money on the table, and stormed out of the sports bar.

All of a sudden, she sensed Gary behind her, gently dabbing lavender on her neck and pulling her head to stretch her neck. It felt relaxing—surprising to have a person touching her—but cool. Jaya wasn't used to the feeling of other people's touch. Her face felt warm from the lavender.

"All right, everyone, please slowly roll back to sitting and open your eyes. Thank you for being a part of this class today. You did a great job. Enjoy your day, your week. Namaste." Gary bowed his head, palms together, towards the class. He was sweating in triumph. Immediately a wispy, thin model type with long blond hair in a ponytail and a proper gap between her thighs walked up to talk to him, looking animated and touching his arm repeatedly. Gary, it appeared, was quite the ladies' man. For the first time, Jaya felt glad that she wasn't encumbered by any desire to catch Gary's attention. Perhaps she could be happy alone for a while, just once in her life. Jaya smiled wryly and bounced down the metal-edged steps, taking care to avoid tripping on her tired feet.

As she walked back to the subway, the effects of the yoga class worked their magic, and Jaya felt incredibly at peace. Her mind—normally a vivid, pulsing, confusing thing filled with plans, half-formed ideas, observations, analyses—was unnaturally calm, as if she couldn't call up a thought if someone screamed fire, let alone have one unbidden. She felt not so much refreshed as she did like a newborn, wiped clean of all mental and emotional plaque. Her wrists shook slightly as she gripped the subway handle on the way home; her arms and muscles were tired, more than she realized. So this was what yoga was all about, she thought. No wonder people get so into it. It was like being drunk, high, happy, and calm all at once. She needed more.

That night Jaya sat propped against the wall on her bed, a mattress with no box spring or headboard, as she balanced a glass of wine on her cheap ten-dollar nightstand. She added a tab to her project management spreadsheet. It was called "Goals and Stuff" and next to it, "Sheet 1" was renamed "Moving Plan."

Though she was excited to make this journey, she was also nervous. Her knowledge of India was limited to interactions with her parents and their friends, who had mostly left decades ago, and the various knickknacks purchased on a big trip to the motherland ten years ago, which included embroidered throw pillows that sat in the corner of her room, unused, and a small Ganesh statue that she forgot to pray to daily. What would this experience be like? In her imagination: a bright, orange sun is dropping down to the horizon and she is watching cows being herded home on a dusty road while she sits in a cross-legged yoga pose, breathing peacefully and possibly contemplating going for a cocktail at dusk. Everything is luxurious and at the same time, highly authentic. It's a colonialist's dream. The travel brochure practically writes itself: "Come to India and experience the wonders of a glorious medieval past!"

It now occurred to her, however, that perhaps she would need to consider her personal safety abroad, especially being on her own. Perhaps she had been too rash in agreeing to go along with Daadi Ma's kooky idea. After all, she would be going to a small town where an ashram had been built by apparent money-grubbing yogi types, on land that her family had at one time owned. Would they view her as a spy trying to get the land back? Would they try to fleece her for money? These practical matters were at odds with her musings about this trip so far. But she would rectify this now, in the way she knew best, with a strict set of goals that would inoculate her, in her very calling out of them, from any suboptimal future. She typed into the "Goals" sheet the following list:

Avoid touching people with leprosy (as if)

Do not eat street food

Do not talk about money

No marriage prospect meetups

Satisfied, she grabbed her wine and climbed to the rooftop of her apartment, an off-limits area accessed through a trap door at the top of the stairwell. Contorting herself around the satellite dish that took up too much space, she sat and stared ahead at the winking lights of the helicopters circling near the UN building and sniffed the wafting smell of the garbage below. It was cold up here in a way that she doubted she would feel in the warmer climate of India.

It was odd, she thought, how her mind had changed about this whole thing. Chiefly, she had decided that her family was right. She needed to live a little, do something unconventional. To figure things out, to see things and learn more about her history that she'd always taken for granted. After all, she was a history major. Why not learn her own? But, ultimately, what convinced her was the sheer practicality of it. It was six months, she wouldn't lose money on rent because Mark was moving in with MJ, she could use her savings, and she could always live with her parents if she needed to, to make ends meet before finding another job after she returned. Beyond the practical, she was also frustrated. After all, she wasn't dating anyone so great in New York that it would matter. No one would miss her, and perhaps this would be the thing she needed to change the direction of her life.

Subject: Your Stay at Panditji Kaaju Maharaj (PKM) Ashram

Dear Jaya Ji,

Namaste. We are very much looking forward to your stay with us at Panditji Kaaju Maharaj yoga ashram in Maalpur. As you will be hearing, Panditji Kaaju Maharaj is a very revered man, who has graciously offered this stay, free of charges, to partake in his divine learnings and karmic guidance. While physically demanding, it is also a very rewarding experience to take these yogic challenges and you will find it brings one closer to God in our ancient traditions. Your great-great-grandfather, J.L. Gupta, may Bhagvan rest his soul, was a great patron and donated his land most auspiciously to build this ashram which now houses up to 100 devotees at any time and provides needed service to the poor and the women and the cows. As you have kindly reverted the details of your trip, we have arranged transport from the Maalpur station when the train arrives on Saturday morning, at 10 a.m. sharp, or if the rains are coming, then between the hours of 11 and 3 p.m.

All the best,

Lilly, Ashram Manager

CHAPTER THREE

The Ashram

On the plane, somewhere above the Atlantic, Jaya floated in an imprecise and hazy location. She'd saved the guidebook for this journey, and now she was finding out that her grandfather's birthplace, their family's land, was the site of what appeared to be the only game in town.

Maalpur (Map, p. 34)

Maalpur is a quiet town off a train station. You're likely to stop here on a train journey to somewhere else. While you're at the train station, check out the colonial-era murals, now sadly in slight disrepair, painted by a leading 17th-century French artist during the age of the British Raj. There is one decent cafeteria serving fried snacks, or you can do as the locals do, and sample the fare from the food carts that hover outside. The main attraction is a yoga ashram, run by Panditji Kaaju Maharaj, who claims to have over one million devotees; daily tours and drop-in meditation sessions cost Rs 250, with additional yoga mats, showers, and a change of clothes available upon request for an added fee. To get around Maalpur, the best choice is an auto rickshaw or taxi from the train station to your destination. There are two hostels nearby, but most travelers will prefer to rent rooms from the yoga ashram if they can swing it, for Rs 1,000 per night, or Rs 2,000 per night for a single room. Near the train station, the unremarkable and slightly dingy YM guest house charges Rs 500 per night for a shared room or Rs 850 for individual rooms.

"Wow, all that's in Maalpur is the yoga ashram," she said out loud, forgetting where she was for a moment. In the window seat, her snoring neighbor, a woman in a burqa, shifted when she heard the noise, readjusting her fabric and her bare feet which were pressed against the wall. On the other side of Jaya, in the aisle seat, someone was listening to her and watching her.

Jaya felt the presence and looked up. He was about her age, and not bad looking. "Did you want a water?" he asked. "I took an extra one earlier when you were asleep." He smiled and shifted the small plastic bottle from his tray table to hers. How thoughtful. Surprised, Jaya smiled back and noticed how her seatmate's curly, dark hair was flopping in multiple directions. It looked somewhat greasy from the stale air on the plane.

"I'm sorry, did I hear you say Maalpur?" he asked, squinting in the direction of her travel book. "I'm not sure I've been to that part of the country, yet."

"That's right," Jaya said, slightly embarrassed that he'd heard her. "Maalpur. It's in Madhya Pradesh, sort of in the middle... I'm going to a yoga ashram there. Well, it's sort of a long story."

"We have a lot of time," her seatmate said. He was looking at her with interest. "I'm Josh, from New York."

"Jaya, also from New York." Maybe, she thought, she wouldn't need to worry about meeting people, after all.

"Maalpur. Yoga ashram. Panditji Kaaju Maharaj, am I right?" Josh said.

Jaya's eyes widened. "Yeah, you've been?"

"Uh, no. Not yet. I just heard about it. A friend of mine went there a few years ago. He came back twenty pounds lighter and vegan."

"Oh wow. Well, I'm not going there to lose weight, but that would be a nice side benefit. So, why are you headed to India?" Jaya said. "If you don't mind my asking."

"Actually, I'll be there, I mean here, indefinitely. For research," he replied, not sure if he should go on. Josh was suddenly conscious of Jaya's long straight black hair and pretty green eyes; he wondered if his hair was totally out of control, just based on the way she was looking at him. He tried to act casual, but cursed internally as he flubbed his answer. He was sure the whole thing came out much more declaratively and seriously than he'd intended.

"Oh, research. What sort of research?" Jaya asked.

"Actually it's a bit obscure," he said, his enthusiasm returning. "A study of the Russian language's roots in Sanskrit. Do you speak Hindi? I'm sorry to pry, but..."

"No, no worries. Yes, I do. But what does Hindi have to do with Sanskrit and Russian?" She could see that he had something to say, as his eyes brightened and got more intense. It was clear this was someone who passionately believed in what he was talking about.

"So, as I learned, and you probably know this already, Sanskrit is the root of Hindi," he said.

"Yep, but very few people actually speak Sanskrit."

"Well, they did way back. The Russian language is actually a proto-Indo European language. Which means..."

"Which means it's rooted in Sanskrit, is that right?" Jaya finished his sentence.

"That's right!" He lowered his voice, conscientiously, when he noticed the woman sleeping next to Jaya shift in her seat. "Anyway, I'm going to research the connections between the two languages—like really get into the roots of it. The whole idea is to do it using comparative literature, finding texts from those times and comparing word similarities."

"That's not something you hear every day," Jaya said. Her mind felt like it was expanding, just talking to him, and she was energized by the whole conversation. "I'm just a project manager for an insurance company. Well, *was* a project manager. It wasn't that exciting. But it doesn't matter anyway, because I am not there anymore. I'm between jobs, as it were, so now I can do things like this."

Josh looked at her with interest. He reminded himself of the promise he'd made to himself before he got on the plane. No more dating, not for a while. Especially, not after the breakup with Lauren. It was too hard to live up to people's expectations. Josh had ended things a week before, as he was packing for India. At the time Lauren was wheedling him about why she couldn't come along. The trip, he had told her, was going to last several months, to produce a new anthology of first-hand research. Long-distance dating didn't make sense: his work was too intense, and it wouldn't be fair to her.

"So what made you decide to spend six months doing yoga?" Josh asked, pulling himself out of his reverie. "That is, if becoming a vegan is not your goal?"

"This came about more because of my family."

"Oh I see... arranged marriage or something, right? I've heard how that's a thing."

"No, no, nothing like that. It's something they asked me to do. To go, I mean. To this yoga ashram for a while. We have a connection to it, in a way." Jaya smiled. Josh was too intense, his dark green eyes boring deeply into hers.

"Well hey, whatever your reasons, I'll be in India for a while, and I don't know many people other than the publisher and his office mates. Would you mind if we stayed in touch? If that wouldn't cramp your style? Who knows, maybe someday I might make it down to this yoga ashram."

Jaya blushed. She hadn't ever met someone on a plane before. But Josh was so focused and direct, that before she could consider her options, she blurted out, "That would be awesome, let's stay in touch, I'd like that."

"Awesome. Well hey, I promise also I'm the real deal. I write a blog. You can follow my exploits on it if you want. JoshRusSansText.com. I'm planning to write about my time in India, the process of my research and stuff."

"Next time I've got internet, for sure," she said while settling back in her seat. She tried to play it cool, even though inside she was feeling the familiar rush of meeting a new guy. Who would have thought?

Someone was already checking into Josh's background. Having freshly purchased his in-flight wi-fi with his corporate credit card, the passenger seated in the row behind Jaya was awake, eavesdropping and bored. The aforementioned website was a jumble of script in different languages, links to academic articles, and small thumbnail pictures of obscure books one could buy, such as *Essays on the Dichotomies Between the Lost Renaissance Principles Texts and the Contemporaneous Writings of St. Bartholomew*. Overwhelmed by the depth of it all, the passenger fell, finally, blissfully asleep, dreaming in a loop about emails unreturned and missed deadlines.

Back in seats 23B and C, Jaya and Josh were locked now in deep conversation about their respective trips.

"I'll be in India for six months, all in Maalpur."

"The whole time?" Josh asked.

"Well, maybe a trip to Delhi or Mumbai to visit some of my grandmother's friends. You?"

"Mostly I'll base myself in Delhi. And after that probably hit up spots where there might be good Sanskrit texts to research."

"Like where?" Jaya was curious.

"Mostly northern India, like Varanasi, Allahabad, Rishikesh and Ayodhya. I'm not sure yet. It's something I'm going to figure out in the next few weeks."

Suddenly silent, they settled back into their little realms, each immersed in their own forward travel plans, staring into the space in front of them, Josh at the inflight screen playing an action movie with a male lead who seemed to be aging in reverse, and Jaya at her open guidebook. Feeling nervous about the next steps in her journey, Jaya reached into her bag for a packet of elaichi, or cardamom, that her Daadi Ma had insisted she carry with her on her travels for nausea. She popped the light green husk into her mouth, chewing on it until the black cardamom seeds released their flavor, relaxing her. In the dark, reading by the dim overhead light, she took out the letter on PKM stationery—which would become Jaya's North Star for the next twenty-four hours—and reread it.

Subject: Arriving instructions to Panditji Kaaju Maharaj (PKM) Ashram

Dear Jaya Ji,

Namaste Om Shanti Om. We are very much excited for your stay in our ashram from the 22nd of April until the 30th of October. For the directions, kindly take from the New Delhi airport any transport to arrive at the main New Delhi Railway Station. Here is your ticket informations:

Train no. 4425

"Inter-India Express"

1 First Class Air-Con

Name: Mrs. Jaya Gupta

LV: New Delhi 2000 Hours

AV: Maalpur 0600 Hours

While on the train please use all necessary precautions. The Maalpur station is a short train stop and you must have your baggages ready as soon as the train stops. There will be ashram greeter and driver at the station for you. How will you know you are in Maalpur? Well, when you begin to see the lush green grass, and the many cows after passing through Agra and Jhansi. Then after Jhansi assemble at the staging area to look for Maalpur signs and if you get to Khajraho you have gone slightly too far. In that case you will kindly call our driver so that he can come get you. Go with God and he will look after you and keep you safe.

All the best,

Lilly, Ashram Manager

The Inter-India Express was waiting for Jaya when she arrived at the Delhi station, and soon she found herself enmeshed in boxes—in her first-class air-con train car, in a long chain of boxy train cars. She was sitting in her berth, in her cabin. Two other passengers had taken the top and bottom bunks. Hours of hustling catching up to her, she zoned out in the fluorescent purple white light, watching the platform start to rush by.

At first the train moved slowly, inch by inch. Then the inches turned to yards as the train picked up speed. And soon the platform was gone and there wasn't anything to see except the blackest of night. As the yards turned into miles, she was carried out of Delhi and into the great vast continent, towards a tiny village her family had once called home.

In her cabin, an elaborate game was underway as the three inhabitants surreptitiously judged one another, taking glimpses at different moments. The shiny-headed businessman in an all-white linen pajama outfit, thick-framed black glasses, and chunky brown sandals was wondering who was this forward young woman from abroad with the audacity to travel alone on a train at night, and thinking how thankful she should be that a respectable couple like himself and the missus were her temporary companions. His wife—fair and heavyset, and crumpled in the cushions trying to sleep in a thin purple-and-orange sari—was wondering why the girl across from her was so thin and that she must be anorexic. Jaya noticed how weary and exhausted the couple's bodies looked, as if they were living in a torpor. She would never understand how people became so tired in older age. Awkward smiles and nods and an errant British-accented "hello" were exchanged, but for the most part, everyone present was engrossed in the most all-consuming of goals: sleep.

Jaya awakened with a start when she noticed that the train had slowed down. Terrified she had missed her stop, she shot up in the berth, knocking her head. Outside on the platform, a boy in shorts rushed up to her window and offered tea for five rupees and she took it. He solemnly pulled out a pottery cup and poured tea in it, steaming hot, from a large kettle and waved to her as he went on to the next window. She drank the liquid slowly, afraid of burning her lips on the clay. Ingenious, she thought, Daadi Ma had told her that these cups was biodegradable, and that after drinking from it, she should throw it out the window. Then, some enterprising person would pick up the pieces and carry it back to a central place, where it would be melted down and refired again into another cup, to feed another traveler, on another train.

A shiver came to her now, as she remembered saying goodbye to Josh at the airport. Odd, she thought. In New York she was just another woman looking for a date, forgettable to guys like David. But now that she had taken off to go hang out at a yoga ashram for six months, people became instantly more intrigued by her. Josh had hugged her goodbye; his hair and hemp smell and light muscles had met her hair and sandalwood soap and the clink of her dangling earrings.

"Well, good luck," he'd said as they exchanged phone numbers in the airport. Josh flipped his hair and Jaya pulled hers back. She'd waved to him one last time as she wheeled her large suitcase out of the baggage claim area.

As the sky lightened, Jaya, now unable to sleep, watched the landscape get greener as the train lumbered past Agra, then

Jhansi, just as the letter from the ashram had said. Jaya felt a rush of panic as she pulled her belongings together, slipped on her sandals, wrapped up her shawl that was doubling as a blanket, and brushed her hair. The instructions said to be ready by the door when the train arrived in Maalpur as it would not stop for long. Luckily for Jaya, the railway signs were big and maroon, with large yellow lettering, showing the place names in both Hindi and English. The train clattered rhythmically on the track for a few long minutes, slowing down and letting her eyes come to focus on the scenery outside: grass, farms, cows, low red-brick walls, people, burning trash piles. Finally, Jaya heard the treble whistle as the train signaled its entrance into a new station. She looked hopefully for the sign to confirm that, in fact, they were in Maalpur. Seeing the large letters, she stepped carefully off the broad steps onto the platform as the train hitched slightly. She took a few steps forward, careful to avoid stepping on the luggage that was stationed all around the platform as others got off the train with her. The platform was already busy at this time of the morning, and unsure of where to go, she stopped and scanned all the strange faces. A white-haired man in his sixties emerged and approached her, putting his palms together in greeting.

"Namaste, Miss Jaya. I am from the ashram. Welcome." Wordlessly her driver pointed to her bags, and two railway coolies in checkered shirts promptly took them from her hands.

"Come, Miss," he said, turning to her. "Your train has been slightly late and you must be quite tired."

Exhausted but feeling invigorated by her independence, without her parents or any other friends, Jaya absorbed the scene around her with a higher degree of focus.

"This you will see, Miss Jaya, is Maalpur," her driver said enthusiastically. "We have many visitors. From all over the world, they come for this ashram! Here, Miss Jaya, here, step over here."

Jaya stepped with agility around a hodgepodge of vehicles assembled in the station parking lot: auto rickshaws, pedicabs, mid-century yellow-topped black-bodied Ambassador taxis, and a few private cars.

"Miss Jaya? Here! Here is the car!" Her driver radiated joy and happiness and a slight sheen of sweat, which he kept wiping off his brow with a small white handkerchief retrieved from his top shirt pocket. Even for ten in the morning, it was stiflingly humid and hot. Jaya welcomed the blast of air conditioning inside the car; she sank into the back seat and closed her eyes in relief. Finally she could relax after all that cacophony and look out the window: narrow streets lined with one-story cement-block shops fully open, doorless, in the front; miles and miles of green fields as far as the eye could see; a sun-darkened woman wearing a thin nylon sari in bright red, with one long end wrapped around her; a man, seated on a wooden pallet, driving a bullock cart.

A few minutes later, her driver, pointed to a modern white building. "See this! You will see our hospital, the biggest in this state. It is even having the most advanced cancer treatment center with the top-class MRI machines. Dedicated to the city by our very own Panditji. He is a very great and holy man. It is said even, that a visit by the Panditji to the sick person can cure the cancer, completely!"

At this, Jaya frowned, perplexed by such a seemingly illogical statement.

"Here, Miss Jaya!" Her guide sat up as the car rattled slightly while crossing a main highway, over a train track and onto a smaller road of packed dirt. "Just up ahead, we are here!"

The ashram was truly beautiful, and she smiled when she saw it. It began with an imposing iron gate at the entrance. Next, a three-story temple dominated her view. The temple was carved in gray stone and built in a traditional Hindu style, with wide steps leading to an entrance walkway. She spotted a large, open-aired gathering hall, where the students practiced, made in the same stone as the temple. And off to the side, a modern, rectangular structure with a white marble façade functioned as the hotel, which housed the guests. Overall, Jaya could see she was arriving at a serious facility for spiritual practice. Determined to make the most of the Panditji's charity, she took a breath to calm her nerves and stepped out of the car to meet the manager, Lilly, who was waiting to greet her with a garland of marigolds in her hands.

"Namaste and welcome to this ashram for yoga instruction class," greeted the instructor sitting at the front of the room. He wore well-fitted white linen pants and a thin white tank top. His dark hair was curly and oiled, bouncing with life. His skin was tanned. By the energy he radiated through the room and the eager looks on the faces of the ten other students in the great hall, she knew this must be the Panditji.

Jaya hadn't expected to meet the reputed Panditji in her very first class.

"Some of you will be here for sixteen weeks. Some for six. Some, like Jaya, for six months. It does not matter," the Panditji intoned. Jaya smiled self-consciously, surprised that he knew her name and her situation. She watched him intently now, curious to learn more about this man who had essentially made her family's obscure hometown an international travel destination.

The Panditji clasped his hands together and smiled in an almost childish way. The kohl which lined the bottoms of his eyes creased into fine lines. His figure was perfect—neither too tall nor too short, neither too muscled nor too thin. "Good! We will have fun together. Now this is my assistant and second in charge, Ravi Kumar. Please say, 'Namaste' to Ravi."

At this, Ravi, an energetic man in his mid-twenties with a killer smile, a dark complexion, and short and high jet-black hair, bowed to the class with his head down and his hands joined.

"Good!" the Panditji said. "Now you are all here because today it is your first day. Now it does not matter to me what or where you are from, how much you know or do not know about yoga. You must check your ego at the door. Today, right now, this will be your first class instruction. My family has been living in this area for hundreds of years. I have learned yoga almost from birth, from my father and his father before him. I started knowing nothing. Just like you."

Jaya twitched a bit at this boasting. Really? Hundreds of years? If what Daadi Ma had said was true, his family had likely been living here for only a handful of years, and most of this ashram would have been built recently. Pushing this thought aside, she returned her attention to the class.

"Now your first lesson in yoga will be about breathing," the Panditji went on. "Breath is the foundation of life. It is the foundation of everything. You, what is your name." He was pointing at a round woman, pale and light-haired.

"Barb, from Texas," she said with a slight laugh, a bit giddy from actually being here.

"Barb from Texas, tell me, when was the last time you thought about your breathing?"

"Um, I'm not sure, really. Maybe at the doctor's office when they asked me to take a deep breath into his stethoscope so they could check my lungs?"

That elicited a laugh from the others.

"Breathing is not something we do only at the doctor's office. It is something we must be conscious of all the time. Now. Let us learn to breathe."

For the next hour, the Panditji was true to his word. All they did that first day was breathe in different patterns. At times, Jaya felt dizzy, as the heat and the jet lag made the long inhales and short exhales harder. She tried her best to stay focused, but her lungs and chest actually hurt, and when she heard the clear ring of the bell, she couldn't help but let out her chest in a sigh of relief.

Within a few weeks of arriving at the ashram, Jaya felt settled in her new surroundings. Her room was the perfect mix of quiet and cool, with a marble inlaid floor, an individual A/C unit, and whitewashed walls. She shared the room with Barb, a blonde from Texas, and Angie, an intense, wiry yogi from Brooklyn. If she wanted privacy, she could sit inside with her headphones on, or if she felt social, she could step into the hallway and talk to any of the other twenty or so students, who had rooms adjoining hers. They would meet in the common area usually every afternoon, to hang out, watch TV, and drink cucumber water. All in all, it was not a difficult adjustment from her life in New York. She missed the bustle of the big city, her friends, and her family, but here, she had a new set of acquaintances, some of whom she was becoming closer to. And of course, there was the yoga.

While logged onto her laptop at night, Jaya had created a new tab in her project management spreadsheet. It was a sign that amid her new regimen of daily yoga, her natural inclinations were coming back: she was slowly claiming control of this new world, piece by piece, with items to be managed. There was muscle soreness—how bad would it be from day to day? She hoped that eventually it would go away as her new buddies Barb and Angie told her it would. And her knee. There was this one pose that required her to twist her knee, and it hurt every time she did it. And her shoulder. It was tight and unforgiving. She hoped to see that over time it didn't feel so much like a joint being popped out. And she wanted to track her mental concentration, which at first was hard to control when she did her daily meditation; her mind wandered, like a goat, as the Panditji Kaaju Maharaj had told them it would, dumb and unthinking. Could she get better at controlling her thoughts with habit? And her breath, which was so shallow and labored—would it open up and become deeper over time? And the sweating—would that stop as she got into shape, so that she wasn't sliding all over her yoga mat in her own drippings? And most of all, could she eventually do a headstand, or even a handstand? No one was asking her to, but if she was ever going to do one, it would definitely be here.

The biggest difference between the ashram and New York, she confided in late night texts to MJ, was this feeling that she couldn't hide anymore. In New York, there was anonymity. Surrounded as you were in a city of millions of people, all living their lives out on the street, with no interest in anyone else, you could be guaranteed complete privacy in the open air. But here, there was no such thing. In the dining room, the ashram's head cook would notice when Jaya took an extra helping, or when she asked for one teaspoon of green chilies instead of two. In the practice hall, Ravi would check her breathing or her posture, and if she had trouble getting into a pose or holding it, she could be sure that he would be there to guide her. And unlike her fellow students, including Barb and Angie, she had not spent four months' salary to be here, and almost everyone knew that it was free for her. She had not chosen to come here to be in touch with her body like Barb was, or to get over a bad break-up like Angie. Jaya was the outlier, someone who was there for someone else, who hadn't paid her way, whose only sacrifice was one she hadn't even made—her family giving up their land to these people some time ago.

And the man himself, the Panditji. She thought about him as well, as she replayed her most recent conversation with him.

"Jaya," he had said, stopping her after the morning practice.

"Yes, Panditji," she said obediently. In his charismatic presence, she was very agreeable.

"As you know, your family contacted me, and this ashram training you are partaking of is free of charge."

"Yes, Panditji."

"I would like—" Here he paused, and stared off into space, then came back and touched her forehead reverently. "I would like for you to come to a special pooja ceremony. This is not, you see, for others. It is something only for those of us who are deeply connected to the ashram, like you. Meet at the reception tomorrow, 4pm sharp. Lilly has arranged it."

Before Jaya could respond with an affirmative, the Panditji had glided off, leaving the scent of sandalwood in his wake.

CHAPTER FOUR

Silsilla's Warning

Daadi Ma had been badgering Jaya every other day on their regular video calls about the state of her hometown and its conversion into the PKM facility. Mostly this was an exercise of piecing together what Daadi Ma remembered from girlhood before the family left for Delhi. Jaya dutifully helped compare the reality that she saw every day with what sat in her grandmother's mind, washed in sepia tones, lying in the same vector of time and space, just set fifty years apart.

"The walls around the area? It was same," Daadi Ma pronounced.

"Long road from Maalpur? It was same."

"Main house? Not same."

"Train station? It was same."

"Ashram yoga area? New."

"Farmland? Same."

"Temple? Same. One time, oh, one time," Daadi Ma picked at a groove in her mind where the memories lay, and she dived in, "one time, there was a bat infestation, in the area. Thousands of bats. Every tree. Every roof. They would come at night and no one safe. We used to, you know, sleep outside on the roof, the chhat, but what to do, these baby bats. Mummy told us all to go inside. Because the bats, they had babies. The babies, they were dropping down from everywhere. Small, like size of your hand. On the radio, it said a factory nearby had by mistake released two tons of fertilizer, which bats ate. And then the bats, they expand. So many all over. Of course, the pujari, the priest, he said it was no factory that caused this. He said this is a bat goddess, a sign from Lord Shiva, that we must pray for them. Well, Silsilla, she was my friend, we were about twelve years old, we thought this priest was very silly. Bats, of course, they are menace. So we gathered up all the small bats and put in burlap bag that stores rice."

Jaya could imagine sixty or so of these bats, some dead, some alive, chirping in the bag.

"And we put them in the temple, in the pooja place. Just the bag, right in front. When the priest came and he saw, he was so mad. So mad. He screamed for the maids to come clean it up." Daadi Ma laughed at this, pantomiming the priest from long ago. "'Who did this?' he said. 'Brought unclean things to God this way?' And we all had a good laugh. Well, not at first. Even my mummy laughed with us, later. She thought it was funny, how scared he was, of the bats. But in front of him, the pujari, our mother gave us girls a big scolding and insisted on cooking him something special that night, to make up for it. Then later she hugged me and Silsilla and laughed and laughed and laughed. This temple, new one, is on same spot. Please go to see Silsilla, Jaya. She still there. She may remember other stories, like this one."

"Yes, Daadi Ma, yes, I will," Jaya replied.

The Panditji's private pooja ceremony was held at dusk in a special alcove off the main temple. In the waning light of the day, the whistle of a passing train rent the air. About twenty people, locals from Maalpur and employees of the ashram, as well as the Panditji and Ravi. Offerings were made, incense was burned, oil lamps were lit. After the ceremony, the Panditji went around offering blessings to each person.

"Jaya, here, you must take the blessings of Lord Shiva," the Panditji said, coming to her last. "God gives us so much, wouldn't you say? Surely, you must, in America, be having a very healthy, wealthy life. It was kind of your family to donate this land, to this temple."

"I suppose, Panditji," Jaya said, uneasy that she was being singled out amongst the devotees. A priest did not usually stop to talk while distributing blessings.

The Panditji continued. "Would you say, Jaya, that your stay here has been comfortable? I wouldn't want you to think that we were not hospitable."

"Of course! It's been... it's been awesome. Learning yoga with you and Ravi has been great."

The Panditji's heavily kohled eyes bored directly into hers, and his hooked nose flared slightly, searching for something. She felt self-conscious and looked down at her brown sandals.

He frowned. "Well, I would not want any of your friends and family to get the wrong idea. This land, for the ashram, you understand now, it is part of something bigger now. No one lays claim to it. Only God. You understand, right?" Smiling now, he continued, "So, because this is for God, please then, please help me. Next month, we'll have the big Shiva Moon Festival. You'll help us, yes?"

"Of course, Panditji," Jaya said. Suddenly, a bat flew from one corner of the alcove to the other. This triggered her memory of Daadi Ma's strange story, about the bat infestation. Could this bat be the progeny of some of those very same bats so long ago? She shivered just thinking of it, and she realized that whatever the Panditji might say, she could physically point to things at the ashram that her family had directly influenced, and so the idea that this place was now some sanitized godly place owned by no one, well, it didn't sit right.

Saturdays were free days at the PKM Ashram. Students could make their own program, while the Panditji and Ravi hosted public classes for the youth. This is how Jaya, Barb, and Angie found themselves crammed together on the back seat of an auto rickshaw intending to hang out in Maalpur proper.

The auto rickshaw slowed as it entered the main town, then came to a stop in front of a movie theater that looked to be in the center of activity. Every inch of street space was claimed— by pedestrian, biker, dog, cow, street vendor, car. It was chaotic but elegant. Using right angles, all those people and objects would not otherwise fit. But somehow, everything flowed, with no discernible order.

The three got out, dazed, and stared in front of them. Several movie posters stared back. In one, a fair-skinned actress lamented her fate while flames blazed behind her, her face a mix of excitement and fear, her hand against her forehead and her head thrown back, her back arched. Her blouse was a mystery, as parts of the movie poster had peeled away, leaving a streaked paper effect. Another poster advertised a cops-and-robbers film, with the hero in the foreground with feathered hair and a shirt opened at the chest, flanked by a policeman in all khaki green and a heavyset bearded villain. Men milled about on the street outside the movie theater, looking at the three female entrants to this scene, unblinkingly and idly.

"Where's your grandmother's friend's house?" Barb asked, shading her pale gray eyes from the sun. She'd forgotten sunglasses.

"Over there, I think," Jaya said, indicating the peach-colored walls of a house off the main square.

"Okay, we'll see you later. We might watch a movie," Angie said.

"Or go shopping. Or just walk around," Barb said.

"See you in a few hours, guys. Be safe," Jaya added, as she rang the doorbell to Silsilla's house.

Moments later, she was sipping a delicious rose water juice drink, perfectly chilled, tickling her throat as it went down. The drawing room—painted in gray-blue limestone and featuring brightly colored stained-glass windows—was a refuge from the chaos of the street. Silsilla herself was a carbon copy of Jaya's own beloved grandmother. She wore the same white sari of a widow, the same low bun, and the same steel-rimmed glasses. Banita, her daughter-in-law, with a wide face and jet black hair, sat on the opposite couch in a stylish gauze sari with her husband Santosh, who was a proper genius at anything electronic but otherwise quite shy when it came to matters of the house. He sat uncomfortably, with their daughter on his lap, the odd man out.

"So, you are Sharmila's granddaughter," Silsilla said to Jaya, studying her kindly. She gripped her cane hard with her elbow pointed upwards, locked into place as she sat. Despite her shaky appearance, Silsilla's mind was clear and sharp, her voice steady and low. "Finally, you come. I told Sharmila, your daadi, to send you to come to us!" She raised her hand as she said this. "She was my old friend," Silsilla continued, before Jaya could even say anything. "We grew up together."

"Tell us, how do you like it? The ashram? Maalpur? It must all be so different for you," Banita added. She had a British accent, sounding rather too sophisticated for a town as small as Maalpur.

Faced with these welcoming people who knew her family, Jaya loosened up a little. "Honestly, it's been an adventure just getting here. The train ride went pretty well, I think? And the ashram is really modern. Oh, and then there's the Panditji, the one who—"

"Oh! Yes, we've heard all about him," Banita said, knowingly.

"Strange man," Silsilla commented, with a bit of snark.

"But tell us, Jaya. You are a career girl, is it? Living in the big New York City, now taking time here at this ashram. It must be so exciting!" Banita said.

Jaya shifted in her seat, feeling distinctly different, as an American, in India. Banita had probably been married before the age of twenty-five, like most other middle-class women in small-town India. It was clear to Jaya that Banita was probably a homemaker, living at her in-laws' house. How different their lives were, Jaya thought. Here she was, independent in all senses of the word, unencumbered by a job, a husband, children.

"You know," Jaya said, "it's nice to be here at the ashram. The Panditji, I mean, his yoga practice is quite spiritual. People come from all over the world to be there. You should come some time."

Banita snorted.

"We stay here," Silsilla said firmly. She leaned forward, toward Jaya. "You, Jaya, you see the ashram, okay. But take care. This Panditji? Who is he? Nobody knows, from where did he come?" She twisted her fingers as she spoke to punctuate the point. "From where did he get this money? From who did he get the land? Who are their people? What is their family background?"

"People talk, Jaya," Banita sighed. "Here in India, this is a small town, not like your big New York City."

Adjusting her sari over her shoulder, Silsilla asked, "Have you met him? This Panditji?"

"Yes," Jaya said, "of course. He teaches us his style of yoga every day, and he leads our meditation. And, well, I can understand your concerns, but I promise he is a world-renowned yoga master, and it's a clean, well-run place."

"What my mother is saying, Jaya," Santosh piped up, "is, please, you are not from here. You cannot trust everyone, and you must be careful. These men who claim to be of God? Always they are corrupt. The power always corrupts. No, —" he turned to Silsilla, "—please do not stop me from saying this. Jaya needs to know."

On the way back to the ashram, Angie and Barb talked non-stop. They were on a high, telling her about the movie they had watched. In it, the heroine wore a perfectly white sari, the hero had a moustache, but they couldn't tell Jaya much more because the subtitles had done a poor job of explaining the plot. They shared with her their leftover popcorn and chips, packaged in plastic baggies and stale from the heat.

Jaya listened with one ear, her mind fixated on what Silsilla and her family had told her. Too many signs pointed to something fairly odd about the ashram. There was a rather hazy understanding of how the Panditji had come to the scene. Silsilla seemed to think he had appeared out of nowhere. Daadi Ma's explanation of how her father had lost the land indicated that someone had poached it. True, it was exceedingly common in

India to lose land due to squatters, but then the Panditji himself lied about, or at least embellished, his historical connections to the property. Then there had been his strange comment, Jaya recalled, about how her family had no claim to the land, because it was actually God's. None of it made sense.

Still, the ashram's living quarters, with their marble floors and air conditioning units, were a dream to return to after a grimy afternoon in town. Jaya and Barb followed Angie to their room, where they were thinking of practicing their yoga postures. Earlier, Lilly, the almond-eyed Bengali ashram manager, had stopped Jaya at the entrance. "Oh, Miss Jaya. You have a message. A phone call came, for you. From Delhi. Josh, I believe his name was. He said to tell you to call him. He said you would have his number."

"What?!" Barb reacted first when Jaya told them. "Who is *Josh*?", dragging the name out with her Texan drawl.

"Oh, a guy I met on the plane," Jaya said.

"Well, it's about time there's a bit of romance around here!" Angie yelped as she hung upside down in a handstand, the veins in her forearms popping out slightly. She could hold the stance nonstop for hours, making the others a bit jealous of her form. With legs neatly tucked and arms perfectly sinewy, Angie was a veteran yogi of the PKM Ashram. "I mean, besides the ultimate romance," she added. "You know, right?"

Jaya and Barb looked blankly at their friend—well, at a mass of dark curly hair covering their friend's upside-down face.

Angie blew a lock of hair out of her mouth. "Panditji and Ravi, of course. You know they are lovers?"

"Wait, what?!" Barb said. "I didn't know? Was I supposed to?" After eyeing Angie, she crouched down on the floor to get into a handstand, willing herself to try to hold one at least a minute before flopping back to the ground.

Barb was the complete opposite in body shape to Angie and had come to the ashram to lose weight. In Dallas, she had tried everything, even stapling her stomach. And nothing had worked. So she wrangled one month off from her boss at the real estate company, who had raised his bushy white eyebrows when she had asked him, told her not to drink anything funny when she was over there—and to come back soon to her receptionist's desk. At twenty-six, she was committed to making good on her college degree and had tried, for a few months, to apprentice as a real estate broker. But the stress had driven her to eating. It was the nerves, her mother had said, that caused her to gain weight, so much so that she almost popped her lap band. Something had to change. When she saw a flier for the PKM Ashram, she thought, "Why not yoga?" And here she was.

"Oh yeah, okay, I guess I see it now that I think about it," Barb continued thoughtfully, "but that's too bad. I kind of thought Ravi was cute."

"Well, you know the Panditji," Angie said. "I mean he's a control freak, so he's super careful about who knows what. I only know because I've been coming here forever, and it wasn't until the third year that I found out."

It was Jaya's turn to get into a handstand. She concentrated as she maneuvered her body to flip up against a wall.

"But anyway," Barb piped up, not willing to be distracted, "who is this *Josh*?"

"So like I said—a guy I met on the plane," Jaya said through gritted teeth from sheer focus. Her handstands were getting there, with Angie's coaching. "So he's from New York but now here like me, and he's an editor trying to publish a book about Russian language and its roots in India. I think he said he is based in Delhi. I mean, he was super interesting to talk to."

Angie perked up at the prospect of blossoming love. She was a romantic at heart, despite her break-up last year. They always say divorce is bitter, but in Angie's case, this was not an expression but a fact. After her divorce, caused by nothing so exciting except a gradual distancing of the heart, her stomach felt like it was coated in a patina of sickly yellow green, leading to a dangerous loss of appetite and weight. The low point was on a random Thursday night, when she had gotten a sealed envelope containing a hefty check covering two years' worth of living expenses. Her ex had sent it to her in exchange for their dogs, which he said would be better off in his new, fancy waterfront condo with an acre of greenspace on the roof. It irked her that her ex and his new wife's money could do this, but it was the right thing to do for the dogs. Soon after, she called up her friends at the PKM Ashram and booked a vegetarian stay. Already, her color had returned from eating a plain diet of lentils and rice.

"And?" Angie asked Jaya. "And what?"

"Cute?" Barb prodded.

"Oh, definitely, in a nerdy sort of way," Jaya said, smiling, coming back to a seated position. Despite herself, she remembered the hug at the airport when they'd said goodbye. The warmth of his body, and his slightly woodsy smell, flooded through her. To get a call from him meant her instincts hadn't been wrong. There *was* something there.

"Why don't you go ahead and call this lover boy back?" Angie said. "Don't worry, Barb and I will be here doing kickass handstands. You can call him back on speaker and we'll determine if he's showing any red flags—or if he really *is* who he says he is."

CHAPTER FIVE

A Detour in Goa

Jaya wasn't in the habit of going to new cities to meet random men. Well, she thought, that was before she'd left her job and started on this whole adventure. If she was going to go off the beaten path, she might as well plunge right into the overgrown jungle and emerge on the coast, in this case Goa. At least Angie and Barb said Josh sounded normal. There was, in fact, a "Josh Hart" online, who worked where he said he worked.

For Jaya, the austerity of the Maalpur and ashram experience—from the rigorous yoga practice to the small town lacking any restaurants or bars—was starting to get to her. So when Josh had suggested on the phone that they take a weekend and meet up in Goa—a place for partying and fun, known the world over to international travelers, no pressure—she'd surprised herself by agreeing. Sooner or later she'd be going back to the real, boring world. For now, it was time to have a bit of an adventure.

She had found the address Josh had given her and was now struggling to drag her rolling suitcase through the sand. As she spotted Josh in a dingy, white plastic chair on the gray beach, two waiters approached to offer help, causing a commotion when Jaya insisted she was fine.

Josh had just cracked open his third beer. The dark brown bottle held a slightly bitter, light ale whose taste was masked with a lime wedge shoved into the top. He felt a drip of sweat make its way down his lower back and swore his beer bottle was sweating too, down its side. He was happy to be here. Goa was, in his opinion, one of the most relaxing places in India. Here, there were bars open all night and partiers without places to be in the morning. Here, there were lazy green palms and sprawling towns. Here, there were fewer people and fewer cars. Feeling relaxed and loose, he stretched his arms over his head.

Before Jaya arrived, Josh was staring aimlessly ahead at the grayish waves crashing soundlessly and at birds hovering around the pieces of food left out on the beach. He watched four dark-haired Israelis wearing tiny black bathing suits playing an elaborate game that involved tossing each other into the water. He watched a large, reddening matron and her mini-me sunburned daughter sitting under an umbrella, reading matching young adult novels. He saw an Indian family of ten, all holding hands, still wearing their pants and saris, wading into the surf and shrinking back as the water soaked their clothes. He gazed at the parade of the blond and the heavyset and the olive-skinned and the braided and the bald, and the sellers of ice cream cones and their eager customers. The past week at the publisher's house had been a nightmare. It was good to get away.

There had been texts, historical texts, that needed to be procured. It had seemed so simple. The last time he had come to India, everything had been laid out for him and all he'd had to do, as the subject matter expert and understudy-in-training, was simply show up, lock himself in a room, and translate and analyze and write. This time, though, he was the senior editor, and it was his job to not only be the expert but also the project leader. And nothing was going to plan. The source books did not arrive. He sat, day after day, on the second floor of a building off Connaught Place in Delhi, at the headquarters of an independent publisher, alongside Mr. Puri, the proprietor, and Amrita, his headstrong, henna-haired daughter. The storefront was surrounded by other independent presses, like finding like over time. As a result, sub-specialties sprung up around this tiny book village. A bookbinder and his apprentice were on the ground floor. A smart blue van, with "A.K. 47 Fast Service Express" stenciled on the side, sat in the parking lot ready to transport books around the city, a service owned by an enterprising retired army colonel. An outlier, the office of a German airline, was the anchor tenant doing steady business with travelers who wore their backpacks like appendages from head to butt.

"See, it is just coming. They are being held in customs," Amrita had said, trying to reassure Josh about the expected texts. "They are coming all the way from St. Petersburg and Germany."

"Can you call, just check?" he had asked with exasperation.

In response Amrita had turned her head and screamed for her assistant. "Lalita!" she yelled. "Please call the customs people immediately for Mr. Joshua!"

Lalita peeked her head out from around her giant monitor. Her face was small and mousy. "Yes, madam," she said and yawned, with all the gumption of the recently sedated.

And they went through the same rigmarole again. He filled out forms in duplicate and then in triplicate, and Amrita called and called and called.

But it was no use. They were weeks late on his project. But in the meantime, he began digging into the books sent to him already, on loan from universities all over northern India. He had spent the last few weeks directing a recent college grad in philosophy, to catalog the books and make an outline, from which they could determine which titles were needed for the research that would start when the other texts arrived. Frustrated, the next day Josh had booked a ticket to Goa and, on a lark, reached out to Jaya.

"Hey," Josh said now to Jaya, standing up to help her when she and her beach-inappropriate luggage arrived in his field of vision. He caught a flash of her green eyes and thought back to the time they sat only inches away from each other on the plane. He hoped they would be able to talk a lot, and have a lot in common. He really, *really* hoped it.

"Hey, Josh," she said, plunking herself down on the other plastic chair and taking a big swig of his beer. "It is freaking hot out here today. How can you stand it? How can *he* stand it?" She pointed to the overweight gentleman who was patting his forehead with a handkerchief while staring at her with a glazed intensity.

"Also, by the way," Jaya continued, "I'm to tell you that if you display any serial-killer tendencies, I'm to call my friends Barb and Angie immediately." She surprised herself, at her boldness.

"Oh, I could tell you stories," Josh said, secretly relieved. They would definitely have things to say.

A waiter ran over to drop two more cold beers on the table. Clinking their bottles and taking sips, both Josh and Jaya had the same thought running through their minds: maybe this was the best idea ever—and just what they needed.

That evening, they got lost in the Goan night. On a one-lane road, where one-story houses sat peacefully with paper star lanterns hanging on their porches, Josh drove through on his rented scooter, with Jaya riding behind him. The moon glowed in a mostly cloudless, dark gray sky. The scooter was a Josh decision, because he had been to Goa before and his crew had rented several last time. He greatly preferred them to being at the mercy of a taxi driver who would try to sell you hashish. Because that had happened last time, too. A young, red-eyed punk-looking cabbie had once taken Josh for a ride for almost an hour, stopping at multiple hotels and trying to convince him to stay there and get a good discount. When all his attempts had been rebuffed, the driver had demanded that Josh buy hash and, in the end, wheedled forty bones out of him. The hash was in a ball of aluminum foil, which Josh had taken gracefully, rolling his eyes internally. When he opened the foil at the hotel bar, it was empty.

Josh and Jaya were definitely lost now. Surrounded by a jungle paradise: quiet, serene, overgrown. The air was thick and hot and humid. There was no connection to the outside world and no cell service. They were looking for a hotel in the hills named Moon Village that was just quirky and cool enough for dinner. The scooter took a right here. Traveled straight there.

Turned back and went left. All attention was focused here. On the here and now. On the moving towards this place.

Stupid, Josh thought to himself, *you could have chanced a taxi.* But then an image of his dad popped up, and he could picture him telling Josh in his nasal Brooklyn accent to relax and be cool, to let life take its course. Dad was a true believer, a bald-on-top, ponytail-in-the-back free-love advocate, who ran a social-work practice. He worked with kids who had too much and were absolutely convinced their serious deficiencies would prevent them from living whole lives. He worked with kids who had barely anything and freaked out at any sign of the smallest success. Dad ministered to them all.

So instead of cursing because they were lost, he turned around and said, "It feels like when you start a hike. Like when you find the trailhead and you set off, and you look back and you no longer see the parking lot where you left your car, and you can't hear the road anymore, and you're so focused on taking steps forward into the trees or the grass that you get lost in it. And then all you do is look for the trail markers—one to the next. Until you stop looking and just go."

"Yeah, you aren't wrong," Jaya agreed. But behind her agreeable face, she was nervous. *Practical Jaya*, she thought, *doesn't take detours like this. Not without a map.*

They pressed forward together, as real-life explorers. The scooter was a machete hacking through the jungle. In their shared imagination, they were in search of a long-lost pyramid

built by a tribe that had left untranslatable etchings memorial-
izing another time. But the compass wasn't cooperating. Circling back and peering at house numbers and having no active
maps were taking their toll.

Jaya, deciding to take control, said it would be a good idea
to stop where they saw a light a little ways ahead. There were
trucks outside a building there. A stray dog with zero fat
pranced in the parking lot as they neared. A sign read: Kabir's
Restaurant and Dhaba.

Josh slowed the scooter to a crawl and parked it out front.
The joint was busy enough. At least half the plastic tables were
full, with mostly male customers. Some were eating, some were
smoking. One had his head down on the table and was snoring while his companion scrolled through a mobile phone that
uplit his face blue.

"Truck drivers," Jaya said to Josh.

"How do you know?"

"Long-distance truck drivers. This is a dhaba, like a roadside
diner that doubles as a rest stop for truck drivers. Bet they're
coming from up north."

"Ah," Josh said, "I don't think I've come across one of these
yet. You game to try it out?"

"Better this than be lost," Jaya said with determination,
as they shoved themselves awkwardly into the plastic chairs.
"Might as well eat."

"Menus?"

Both Jaya and Josh looked up. A lanky waiter was hovering over them. He had possibly the most insane hairdo Jaya had ever seen, and she suspected she wasn't the first to think this. His crazy, curly hair stuck straight up and out to the side. There were sections dyed blue and sections dyed red. There were small beads weaved in. It created a halo that extended a good six inches in all directions from his head.

"Kabir. Nice to meet you," he said with élan, pulling up a chair to sit next to them and handing them two laminated menus. Small bits of his hair kept moving after he stopped. "This is my place. I mean, this is my dhaba. Welcome."

Kabir confidently snapped his fingers in the air. Within seconds, a man rushed up with three steaming glasses of milky tea on a tray.

"Please, drink." Kabir expertly lifted his hot glass and sipped. "Mmm..." He wiped his upper lip, and a milk moustache from the curdling milk fat of the tea disappeared. "Where are you looking to go?"

"What gave it away, that we were going somewhere?" Josh joked, deciding that he liked Kabir already. "Josh, from New York," he added, extending a hand.

"Jaya, also from New York."

"Dope," Kabir said, and he raised his tea glass in the air to toast. Two more glasses rose in unison. "Really, where are you trying to go?"

"It's... I guess it's not important. Some place called Moon Village?" Jaya said. "But, um, we don't have any phone service out here, so we'll never find it."

"But now you are here, right? Do you eat non-veg?" Kabir asked.

They nodded, hopeful and hungry.

"Bhaaiya!" Kabir yelled. A cook in thick leather sandals ambled out to their table. Slight and bowed and wearing a dun-colored tank top, he held a short notepad against his incongruously protruding belly. As Kabir passed along their order, the cook noted it down using a gleaming gold ballpoint pen. He nodded, focused mostly on the floor and his pen, as if the concentration of listening and writing was the most that he could commit to this social exchange.

The cook's general shyness did nothing to hint at what would come out of his kitchen. Rich flavors and bursting colors appeared on stainless-steel plates. It is easy to make friends, at any table, anywhere in the world, when dishes of butter chicken and garlic naan and marinated red onions are placed in front of you.

Jaya loosened up as her hunger subsided. Even though this was an unplanned stop, now that they were here, she was trying to make the best of it.

"So, Josh," Kabir started, making conversation, "what is it like in New York? Actually, of course this is my father's place, but someday I want to work in advertising on Madison Avenue—this is my dream! I am taking my courses to become a design and graphic artist now."

"It's... it's just my home. You can find anything there. Any type of person. Any kind of food. There's always something going on. Like, at two in the morning, you could find a group of teenagers dancing on the subway."

"That's cool, man!" Kabir said. "Here, Goa is you know, it's more chill. It's mellow—we all just hang out and live. And you and Jaya, you're friends from back home?"

"Not exactly," Jaya jumped in. "Actually, we met on the plane, on our way over here."

"Wow, okay!" Kabir said, sizing up Jaya again. It wasn't a look of judgment, though, but one of slight admiration.

"We, that is," Josh continued, "we both came here for projects. Me, I'm here in Delhi for a book that I'm editing. I study languages, like Sanskrit and Russian."

"And I'm hanging out at a yoga ashram for six months. But, um, not because I'm trying to find myself or anything, it's, well, Daadi Ma forced me," Jaya said.

"Oh I get it, Indian grandparents, huh? So pushy," Kabir said.

"So pushy sometimes," Jaya said, smiling to herself, thinking of Daadi Ma and wondering what she must be doing right now. She pictured her sitting in her corner of the couch, needling her mother to keep the channel on her favorite soap opera, an ongoing serial about infighting between a mother-in-law and daughter-in-law. It caused Kiran an endless amount of grief, and she swore Daadi Ma used it as a passive-aggressive cudgel to guilt her into being more dutiful.

"Sorry." Jaya realized she'd spaced out. "So what's new in Goa? Like, what's the latest?" she said awkwardly. "Josh actually has been here before, but me, it's my first time."

"Latest?" Kabir repeated. "Nah man, here, there *is* no latest in Goa. Here, this is beach life. Jungle life. You know. Simple life. Good life. Actually," he paused looking at both of them, "you guys are cool, right? I'm heading somewhere tonight. If you want, you can come with me? Goa style. Come, na?"

Josh looked at Jaya. Jaya looked at Josh. She nodded her head yes. He arched his eyebrow. A signal passed betwixt them, unspoken. Language is irrelevant when two people are sharing a similar experience. This is the traveler's code: you're here now, so you might as well try something new. It starts with one thing that seems plausible and risk-free and normal: a job. A defined period of apprenticeship and study. And then it slowly fractals out. Here you are, attempting to speak languages you do not know. There you go, taking public transportation at godforsaken hours of the night from airports in cities you've never been to. The next thing you know, you're making friends with just anyone, people you meet on the beach, or on the plane, or at a bar, simply because they are sitting next to you. Anyone in this world of six billion could brush past you, and you'd consider giving them the time you have and your attention. Because you have it. You have no meetings or phone calls or chores. You have nothing to do but talk to this stranger. Then you're having fun, in this stranger's new world and it seems like a good idea to get lost inside the hedonism of it, the third cocktail, the deserted beach party, the random detour, as the fractals of risk and fun that are the traveler's code spiral, sometimes out of control. But that was for later in the night. At this moment, they were sitting, at Kabir's dhaba, and they had been intoxicated by the butter chicken and the hell-ya cool of a kid with too much hair and a lot of energy packed into a small-town boy's small-town roadside diner.

In short order, fueled with food, Josh and Jaya piled onto their scooter in the parking lot.

"Follow me," Kabir said as he pulled down his helmet. And he took off, leading the charge on his motorbike. He headed to the right, the opposite direction from where they came. Josh struggled to balance the scooter and move, accelerating as fast as he could to join him. Soon they were in range of Kabir, perhaps ten yards behind him. Kabir had slowed down a bit, to ensure Josh could keep up. They were surrounded once again by almost pitch-black night. Here in Goa, there were few artificial lights.

Though they were going at a good pace, they could not avoid the wet of the tropical climate. A recent, heavy rain had raised the water level of the inlets that flowed in from the ocean, bringing in leaves and branches and plastic bottles and other detritus to block the drains. Near such an inlet, they arrived at a bridge that, from their vantage point, was shaped like a trapezoid—you went up at a steep 45-degree angle, then straight, then down another 45-degree angle.

"Well, that's... brutalist," Josh commented, eyeing the clean lines of the cement bridge, setting his jaw, and preparing to make a go of it.

But before going over the bridge, they faced a large pool of water that had spilled over the road from the inlet. In the darkness, they got off their vehicles and walked motorbike and scooter through the water, then clung as hard as they could to their conveyances as they put-putted them with their determined feet on the gas, going up the too-sharp angle of the trapezoid bridge, then straight, and then too fast down the other side. Predictably, another pool of water waited on the other side, and they all got splashed. Josh cursed, unsure if the engine would survive this second natural barrier. The water, black, unknown, hit the soles of Jaya's sandaled feet and immediately stuck like mud. She dared not look down to see what had happened, for fear of falling off the scooter. During Jaya's moment of panic, Kabir seemed to take this all nonchalantly.

After the bridge, there was absolutely nothing in the darkness. They cruised down an empty road, and all Jaya could see were the shapes of trees and Kabir speeding a little ahead.

CHAPTER SIX

In Da Pub

The sign they saw as they walked in featured "The Pub" in a calligraphic style, on a plaid background and a coat of arms, telegraphing an image of the purest English countryside. To Josh, it brought to mind the classic pubs that he and his family had visited, when Dad had convinced them to take a road trip through England. They drank stouts and draughts alongside the locals even though they weren't yet twenty-one; Josh was only in high school himself.

He said to Jaya, "Don't you think this place would be better named Da Pub? You know? Like instead of The Pub?"

Their eyes fell on the back wall of the bar, where a garish oil painting made to look like a photograph of Bob Marley stared back at them. Bob was looking down, his eyes focused on a soccer ball. Under his right shoulder, a blond woman with dreadlocks was swaying and smiling to the reggae music's beat in real time.

"Mmm," Jaya agreed, nodding at the barkeep. "This certainly has more of a Jamaican vibe than an Indian one."

Ricki, the proprietor of The Pub, had long since added Haile Selassie, Ziggy, and Bob to his pantheon of gods and goddesses whom he worshipped for all things good in this world. Thoroughly westernized and Rastafarian, Ricki was the quintessential Goan scenester. He knew the mafia that kept the big hotel chains running, and their kids and their bouncers and their hangers-on. He knew the rotating crowd of rich French and Israelis who liked to escape their industrialized cities for the colorful and exotic for long stretches of time. He especially knew the local hipsters, many of whom he'd known since they were kids and whom he'd introduced to ganja (a sacred ritual) and beer (always in moderation, never while driving). A benevolent fixer, Ricki was always in the midst of a conversation.

Ricki greeted Kabir when he saw his hair coming through the iron-gated door. He wasn't surprised to see people follow him in. Kabir was rarely alone. And he almost always came by on Saturday nights.

"How you?" Ricki said in his Indo-Jamaican accent. "Red Stripe, okay?" Without waiting for them to respond, he reached into a refrigerator behind him and grabbed three cold bottles, spinning them out on the wooden bar so that they slid a little bit. "On da house, friends of Kabir, from?"

"New York," Josh and Jaya said at the same time.

"New York, cool," Ricki said, extending a hand to Josh, and nodding at Jaya. "On da house. Sit. Enjoy my pub."

Jaya raised her glass, clinking it with Josh's, and reveled in the deep irony of the moment she was experiencing. In fact, they were both slightly dazed by the dichotomous scene—this reggae paradise in a staid English wrapper—and watched Ricki bop his head to the music as he moved with high energy around the bar area. He was a short man, and his head was barely six inches above the bar counter. Here he was rinsing a glass. There he was pouring a beer. Now he stationed himself to the side of the bar and began to nonchalantly roll a gigantic joint that was almost the size of his forearm. His arms were thick but without muscle definition, as if he had been fed to become stocky and solid from an early age.

Kabir, who was making small talk with Ricki and a thin, equally wild-haired girlfriend whom Kabir had his arm protectively around, beckoned them back over.

"So then I says to her," Ricki drawled to Kabir, "you get out my pub. You no welcome here." He added more leaf to the rolling paper. "No more." Each statement was punctuated by a roll of the joint.

"This gangster's girlfriend," Kabir whispered theatrically to Jaya and Josh. "This guy was making a lot of trouble here before, um, not anymore though," he added hastily, in case they might be worried.

"Yeah, hey, you boyfriend girlfriend?" Ricki asked suddenly, looking up from his task and directing his question at Josh and Jaya. It was an easy assumption, made easier by the fact that both were wearing matching tank tops and shorts and sandals, like they'd planned for couples dress-up night. Ricki whipped out a Chinese-made lighter with the face of Chairman Mao on it, lit up the joint, and took a big drag. He paused a moment.

"I mean," Ricki continued, "it ain't none of Ricki business, but. I like to know who is my customers. Who is my clientele. We get lots of types in dis here place."

"They're cool," Kabir said, with a slight warning tone in his voice. Turning to Jaya, he said, "Ricki just wants to know you aren't troublemakers. Goa, you know."

"Troublemakers? Us?" Jaya laughed a bit, but it sounded more like a hiccup. "Um, I'm a project manager, I mean, I was a project manager until I left my current job, and he's an editor. I'm here at a yoga ashram in Maalpur. He works in Delhi." She shook her hair out of her face.

Ricki watched her carefully as she delivered this. Satisfied that she didn't seem to be a rich kid or police plant or worse, he handed her the joint, to which she shook her head "no." Ricki shrugged and passed it to Josh, who took a small and then a bigger puff. Holding the joint out to stare at it, he raised his eyebrows in appreciation.

"Good shit, right?" Ricki said.

"The best," Josh said after exhaling, truly meaning this, passing the joint to the next person. Kabir took a large drag and passed it to his girlfriend, who did as well.

Just then, the music started pulsing—loud, insistent rap. Kabir and his girlfriend, who still hadn't been introduced, rushed out to the dance floor, throwing their hair around with abandon.

"I think we've been ditched," Josh said to Jaya, nodding at Kabir.

"I don't mind," Jaya said. "Tell me something about yourself." She was firing up a project spreadsheet in her mind. New row, old problem. Category: finding a boyfriend. After the meeting on the plane and the hasty plans they made to travel to Goa, Jaya thought the verdict was still out on whether he would materialize into enough of a prospect to warrant a row. But, somewhere between his telling her about his family in Brooklyn and growing up in Prospect Park and going to college, she decided he deserved a row. Plus, he was cute, with that crooked smile and the longish hair and the thin but muscular build.

"So what's the weirdest thing you've seen so far, at this ashram that you study at? I mean, aside from the obvious," Josh asked.

"Well," Jaya paused and thought for a moment. Took a sip of her beer. "Maalpur is traditional," she finally replied. "But

I guess it's so traditional, it's weird? Like a traditional Indian village out of the past. And the ashram is—I guess—good but it's like, almost too perfect? I don't know how to explain it."

"Okay...." Josh encouraged.

"So the ashram is really beautiful—they have this big Shiva temple that does all these things for the villagers, you know? They feed them and host religious ceremonies. And the ashram itself is amazing. The Panditji practices his own type of yoga. It's neat. Like, he created his own yoga system. Aside from the fact that I've lost ten pounds since coming here, the place is so full of peace and quiet. It's wonderful and relaxed and chill. I'm learning a lot and it's amazing. But how can I say this? It seems disconnected from reality. It's so clean and perfect. Like a utopia. And outside, the world is full of poor people with no electricity, and people who don't have jobs and things aren't squeaky clean. And then there's the weird part.... How do I even..."

Jaya looked into his eyes and decided she could trust him.

"Okay, so Josh, here's the thing. My family actually used to own the plot of land that the ashram sits on. Did I mention that?"

"Maybe you did, on the plane? I guess I assumed it was some kind of birthright trip. But what does the land have to do with anything?"

"So okay, I told you a little bit but not the whole story. But this is the part I didn't tell you—I guess it's nice that I can talk to you because I've not been able to talk to anyone about this—maybe it's nothing. Maybe, I..."

"Get to it," Josh said, pushing her bare shoulder in a friendly way. A thrill ran up Jaya's arm. She smiled, feeling comfortable enough to continue.

"So, anyway, this yoga guy, Panditji Kaaju Maharaj, that's his name, right? He basically claims that this land is his ancestral home and that he's been living there forever, like his family has been there hundreds of years. Which isn't possibly true. But he says it in front of me. I know for sure that my grandmother lived there before. And she told me about what the land used to be, and it's not what the Panditji is describing. And that wasn't hundreds of years ago. That was not even fifty years ago. And then my grandmother's friend, I went to visit her, and she told me the strangest story—about how the Panditji showed up one day and no one knew where he came from."

"Huh." Josh looked stumped. He flipped his hair and picked at his shoulder through the tank top.

"Sounds like a mystery," Ricki piped up from the bar. Jaya hadn't realized he was listening. "My man, Dan Katt, he's a famous hunter of mysteries. Filming a reality show in India, ya? You want, I put you in touch with him."

Josh looked up "Dan Katt" online, saw that he looked like a younger, punk-rock version of Indiana Jones, with a jaunty hat and a multi-zippered khaki vest. "This guy, right?" Josh held up his phone.

"Dat's him," Ricki said. "You want, I put you in touch?"

"Would it help?" Jaya asked.

"Tell you what I think," Josh said, "maybe this Panditji's one of those guys who thinks, you know, creating a mystery will give him a better story. Make him more money. He sounds like a talker. You know? Maybe this Dan Katt character could look into it?"

"That seems rather drastic," Jaya said, a bit alarmed. "I wasn't really thinking of doing anything with this information. It's kind of 'it is what it is'. And anyway, my grandmother doesn't care. Chances are, she'd be more thrilled to hear about you than the weirdness at the ashram."

"Of course it's your call," Josh said quietly and seriously, surprising her. "But from what you've told me, I think this guy's lying. You know that, too."

"I mean..." Jaya felt as if she had to defend the Panditji and, by extension, her situation.

"I just mean that, in all the time I've spent reading and translating ancient texts, the one thing that strikes me is how frequently men of god were like the CEOs of ancient times," he continued. "They ruled with complete power. Just like now, people give them power—willingly—in exchange for something else."

Chills ran down Jaya's spine. What Josh said had a ring of truth to it. Wasn't that what she was doing in Maalpur, hanging out with the yogis who traded in the acquisition of power through their practice? It all seemed a little more than she'd bargained for, especially a few months ago, in the kitchen with Daadi Ma, when the ashram was just a distant notion and the idea of living there for six months seemed a harmless bit of fun.

In the wee hours of the morning, as Josh and Jaya left Kabir and Ricki and The Pub to make their way back to the main road, on murky directions and an unsteady grip, through an empty Goan night, they talked. Josh was insanely curious to hear about her, and Jaya was loosened enough to comply. After all, it was their first date.

The scooter ride became a game of flirtation. Jaya pinched Josh's side. Then he pinched hers back. Then they were laughing with Jaya's arms wrapped around his. It wasn't long until Josh pulled over, turned around and planted a kiss on her lips. They continued like that, stopping every mile or so, to kiss and touch. Haltingly, they returned to their hotel, where they clambered to the back where the beach was and sat on a log in the moonlight. It was the smell of him that got to her: like soap and some indescribable thing that could only be thought of as male. It was her hair that got him: scratchy and sleek at the same time, brushing against his shoulders.

The devil that was her conscience kept Jaya from going too far though. She wondered if the hotel staff saw, if they laughed at her for her transgressions against proper womanhood. She couldn't do this. Not with someone she barely knew. But in the end, she simply exhausted herself after the night of driving about and dancing and drinking, and she found herself awake around 5 a.m., listening to the sound of a crow while still lying in Josh's arms on the beach. He was asleep. She slipped out of his grip, and he adjusted without waking.

That morning, despite her exhaustion, Jaya practiced yoga on the sand. Saluting the sun, she was at one with the oldest yoga tradition in the book, and it made sense because yoga always starts in the dawn just as sun rises. And then it began. Rise up. Sweep down. Lift up. Jump back. Push down. Lift the head. Swing back. Hop. Again. Rise up. Sweep down. Lift up. Jump back push down lift the head swing back and hop and rise up. The poses took over, while Jaya's hair flipped and stuck to her shoulders as she began to sweat. She felt a bead of sweat trickle down her back during a forward bend. She felt the sides of her shoulders stretch as she moved sideways. She felt arm muscles sorely aching and leg muscles stiffly stretching, and her neck, always her neck, moaning in pain, while her lower back breathed a sigh of relief in plow pose. And then it was done. Savasana. Lying flat in the sand, she felt her body drop, heavier and heavier, down through to the other side of the world, probably down to a beach in Brazil where the seasons were flipped, while her soul fluttered, light and lighter out of her chest to a place right above and outside of her body. The sand stuck gently to her shoulders and neck, tickling. She sighed. Her mind cleared. She smiled. She felt a part of the world. A part of the earth. Indifferent to time. Indifferent to history or being or bearing. Then, a cloud came over her and a pang of anxiety. She remembered the Panditji, and the ashram, and the upcoming Shiva Moon Festival. She sighed, not looking forward to returning to the ashram, but unsure as to why.

CHAPTER SEVEN

Rocking Out

To: Daadi Ma

From: Jaya

Subject: The Shiva Moon Festival

Hi Daadi Ma, how are you? The latest here is that the night of the full moon is coming up, and preparations for the Shiva Moon Festival are keeping us busy. Do you remember it, from your time in Maalpur? It's an impressive amount of work to scale up the space and accommodations of the yoga ashram for this many visitors. My friend, Angie, the one I told you about, who's been here before, she told us that the annual festival has gone from a small religious ceremony attended by a few hundred local devotees to, in just five years, an international event attended by thousands, with TV coverage and everything. Can you believe that? I think, being at the ashram for this event will be something to remember, and I can't wait to come home and tell you guys all about it. Oh, and the Panditji, he asked for my help during the festival. I'm pretty excited about it actually. I'll write more about the Shiva Moon Festival once it's over. And yes, I will take pictures!

As with the festivals in prior years, Ravi was on point to deliver this spectacle once again. He imagined smartly suited people in impossibly snowy cities, watching his festival on TV, wearing serious grays and blues, sitting at plastic breakfast tables, drinking coffee like they did in commercials. It was morning, and Ravi was already rushing about, daydreaming as he walked crisply towards the kitchen to heat up the Panditji's tea. He shook his head to push out the sleep and stirred in exactly two teaspoons of sugar into the tea.

Ravi was, this morning, as he had always been, a loyal assistant to the Panditji. Equal parts butler, lover, and assistant yogi, he existed to serve only the Panditji and his needs. This had been the case ever since he was fifteen years of age, when his parents had made a gift of him to the ashram. It had been an occasion more filled with hope than abandonment, one that

Ravi had enthusiastically advocated for. He had been blessed with good looks and a deep voice, which as a shy person, he used rarely. In Ravi's corner of the world, farmers were by necessity uneducated and often deep in debt, buffeted by the whims of the rains and the soil. Being given to the ashram was akin to being nominated for a priestly calling. While spartan, the ashram promised education and learning and a higher purpose. At first, Ravi had visited his parents' house every Saturday evening. But gradually, the intervals between visits lengthened from weeks to months. The difference in attitudes between his parents, who were uneducated, often exhausted farmers, and the self-righteous yogis was too great. Thankfully, Ravi's essential estrangement did not leave a lasting pain in his heart. Because of his relative quiet, he was affixed with universally well-liked qualities. He was viewed as loyal and good-hearted, and was generally well-suited to the role of an assistant. His mother had been proud of him in the end. Her guilt over having to give him up, for some debt now long-forgotten, never left her. When she passed, Ravi came to her side to hold her hand one last time. Even then, she was a stranger to him. For his father, who was incapable of supporting his mother, and who spent most of his days listlessly staring at his fields, drunk on homemade alcohol, he held nothing but contempt. Ravi was happy to move on in his new life as a yogi, and the lover of a powerful man. In his heart, he was content with his lot in life, and loyal to the Panditji. Ambition was a seed that never took root.

Now he went, machine-like, walking fast in short, brisk steps through the main hallway that opened onto the central open-air courtyard, to bring the Panditji's steaming hot tea to him before the morning's first light.

"Panditji," Ravi said, walking into the bedroom carrying a compact black tray.

The Panditji, who took the cup with his pinky held up, was seated on a wicker chair near the window, watching the sun break through the sky. He had earlier awoken in a state of frustration, thinking about the Shiva Moon Festival. Every year it was the same. For all the breathless reviews of the beauties and traditions of the occasion, he felt that the organization, the planning, the innovation required to keep it going was not well understood.

"Tell me, Ravi, how are the preparations?" the Panditji asked. The Shiva Moon Festival was not an ancient tradition that had arisen tree-like, out of the ground, organically from the native soil to naturally take its rightful place in the world. It was a modern, mass-produced spectacle with a budget and a plan. The Panditji felt that no one truly appreciated what he had done for the world, creating an entirely new form of yoga practice and reinvigorating the festival. No one understood except for Ravi, he sighed. Ravi, who had been with him every step of the way.

"Certainly, Panditji," Ravi replied in his low voice. "Actually, sir, Tommy has driven twenty guests just yesterday coming from the train station." Tommy was the perpetually annoyed driver, who had been running continuously between the ashram and the train station to ferry the international and national visitors returning to Maalpur for the annual festival.

"And Lilly? How are the accommodations?"

"All is as planned," Ravi said soothingly, shaking his head from side to side. Lilly had found space to house ten families, two single adults, and ten youths. Fifteen telephone messages sat neatly in a pile on her desk, messages received from other former students of the Panditji.

"And the tents?"

"They are there, sir," Ravi said. These were the tents that Lilly had procured from the local army commander, who had his men install them and portable toilets throughout the grounds in exchange for a special blessing during the ceremony.

"Food?" the Panditji asked. "Feeding the poor, the poor must be treated with respect."

"Of course. Cook has all the cookers going now." These were large brass vats that were used just for this once-yearly occasion. The vats had been brought out of hibernation, and given a thorough cleaning, and were now filled with spices and tomatoes and other vegetables stewing happily in their own juices.

"Very good," the Panditji said, satisfied. He sipped the last of his tea, handed the empty cup to Ravi, and watched him leave. The Panditji let himself flit into a negative space, seated with his legs crossed and his hands resting on his knees, his eyes remaining closed. It was the air. Thick, hot, and humid, it was the kind of air that made you feel like you were floating. The smell of garbage burning in small fires tickled his nose. The heat rose to bead his forehead as the sun began burning off any remaining fog from the dawn. His wicker chair felt connected to the floor. The cement floor felt translucent, as if he could fall through it to another time, another space to touch his past, buried in layers underneath this very surface. Generations of people with his blood before him had walked this earth, worked this earth, lived on this earth. The Panditji grasped now, for some residual energy that remained of who he had been and what that meant.

From an early age, the Panditji knew he would be a yogi. At eight, he had been apprenticed to the local ashram. For him, there had never been the need for anything else—not family, nor children, nor a wife, nor even friends. He found his purpose and his calling in life with the other men of the ashram. Hard, sinewy men, with discipline and mental clarity, who taught him what he must know of the ancient traditions and how they must be kept alive. As a teacher, he was strict and tough, practicing the same brand of extreme rigor of which he himself had learned. Pushing the limits of physical endurance brought one closer to the point of all of it, which was of course, to become closer to God.

Presently, the Panditji went deeper into his repose, deeper through time and space. His lungs had the strength of a mountain-climber's, as he took one breath after another—in through the nostrils and out through the mouth, on his way to salvation. He was a fish now, swimming in a vast turquoise-green ocean, flapping his gills. He was weightless now, as he once was in his mother's womb. Hot, warm, gloopy, he rolled and rolled in that cocoon.

All the ashram's students were given the day off from yoga practice, and Jaya was assigned to plate duty.

"The masterji, he said you were to help, and I hope it won't be too uncomfortable," Lilly said, apologetically.

Jaya had nodded—of course, of course she would help. Barb and Angie had quickly agreed to help as well. The plates were actually large banana leaves, almost a foot long and half as wide, with a rubbery consistency. They were delivered by a man on a donkey cart, who came with piles and piles of leaves to help feed hundreds of guests. Ensconced at the side of the ashram, swatting flies away and sweating in the morning heat, Jaya, Barb, and Angie were to wash the leaves thoroughly with a hose, then anoint them lightly with oil and turmeric paste. This apparently made the leaves ready to hold food. And, as

Angie pointed out, they were perfectly re-usable as cow feed when the crowds were gone.

It was repetitive, mindless work. Soon, Jaya's back and arms ached. To entertain herself, she watched the gathering crowds. Honking taxis and rickshaws kept depositing more people at the front gates. By midday, as a reddening Barb swore she had to get inside and out of the sun, the ashram grounds were teeming with people in the camping tents, set a few feet apart from one another. In the heat, the devotees were doing an elaborate dance for shade, using the tents as a shield from the sun while sticking strategic parts of their bodies outside to catch the breeze. A woman in a pink sari carried an umbrella to shield herself. There were families and children and bearded, half-naked holy men and international backpackers and former students. Above all that humanity, the temple shimmered, its steps recently washed and its façade hosed off so that its stone gleamed a dark gray. Flowers hung brightly in straight garlands, accentuating the holy place.

Before the sun set, Barb came back full of information.

"There was a fight," she announced. "The Panditji and Ravi, oh man, they really went at it!"

Jaya looked up from her work, eyes wide.

"Oh yeah," Barb continued. "Ravi was trying to get more tents set up, but the Panditji was just not having it, and insisted that there were too many people here this year and that the extras be sent to stay somewhere else. Actually, I guess it wasn't very nice. Those people came all this way, right? Ravi said that if the tents were put up outside the ashram, they would be vulnerable to wolves and stuff. The Panditji said he didn't care, that even if a few people were harmed, he couldn't handle the overcrowding."

Angie shook her head. "Unfortunately he's kind of a control freak. Thinks he's a god. I've seen him get like that before."

Jaya said nothing, but inside she didn't feel quite right. This Panditji was powerful, and he seemed to run the ashram with total control. Thank goodness she was just a visitor, she thought. She didn't need to get involved. Right now she could focus on the festival: tonight the worshippers would pray at the temple and then be fed, eating in rows on the floor. Even as she thought this, vats of food simmered, waiting to be spooned out.

Later that evening, Jaya was standing with her friends in the middle of the temple. They had a good view of the action upfront, including of the large Shiva idol and of the priests in white cotton dhotis wrapped around their waists and their hair in buns. They were readying flowers and milk and water, singing hymns as they prepared for the ceremony. Jaya saw Ravi out of the corner of her eyes. He was running around the back area, passing things to the priests.

And she saw the Panditji arrive, looking resplendent. His hair was shining and oiled, his eyes sparkling jet black. He was wearing a full, white cotton long-sleeved top and pants with light embroidery in the same white thread adorning it. He was removing his shoes, stepping into the altar area. He was bowing deeply to each priest, who in turn tapped his head in benediction. He was taking his seat upfront in a position of preeminence.

As Jaya and the audience stood, the space shrank. More people were arriving from behind, pushing them forward. Jaya turned to see the sun, a pink ball, slip down the horizon as she heard the echoes of a train on the nearby tracks whistling through. Small oil lamps began to come into focus amid the darkening sky. A droning chant began from nowhere, carried on a light breeze, buttressed with bells and gongs. The ceremony had started. The priests threw flowers, rice, milk, and water into a fire in front of the Shiva idol. They chanted. They prayed.

As she watched, Jaya was struck by a new feeling. The ashram and her daily yoga practice were serene. She grasped for grace each time she sat to meditate, practicing a spirituality that combined the essential ethos of a spa and the rigor of an educational institution. Together, they taught the theory of how to live life mentally and spiritually. But here in this place, the way that religion was being celebrated now was decidedly different, with priests chanting unintelligibly in hypnotic Sanskrit, while pouring rounds of water and milk, and throwing flowers and rice on a black stone idol; people crowded elbow to elbow, hair bun to face. There was no personal space to reflect, to grow, or to contemplate. The objective might just be to merge the physical presence of oneself with the divine, to remove the need for personal space, to remove the need to think, to remove the need to feel anything. You just needed to stand and be entranced by what was happening in front. It was a big, devotional rock concert, with its attendant physical discomforts and sounds that overpowered an individual's feeling of the self and allowed one to connect into the larger whole. How very different were the approaches to experiencing the unknowable. Yoga was a personal, intellectual, and physical quest for the sublime. Ritual, a deliberate physical experience mashing up one's personal body and mind to sublimate it to something else.

The physical took over Jaya now, as she felt a slight push from the right and a tug from the left. Uncomfortably smashed into place by the people around her, having trouble even breathing in the heat, she tried to make her way to the side to get closer to Barb and Angie. She could see a small spot next to the stone pillars, and she weaved her way towards it. The ceremony began to wind down, and the priests invited the crowd to come up and take the blessings of the gods.

Without warning, the crowd surged forward, knocking Jaya sideways. She was pushed further to the left, into a door whose handle jammed painfully into her side rib. She realized in shock, that she might even have drawn blood. Another loud gong started, and the audience made a collective noise and began to push even harder. Smarting from the pain in her side, with tears in her eyes, Jaya, without thinking, tugged the door open and was shoved into the opening. The crush of people pressed the door on her back and slammed it shut. Immediately, she pulled the handle to try to force her way back into the main room. She couldn't, though. The door didn't budge.

Okay, no big deal, Jaya thought, sizing up her new surroundings. *This must be the back area of the temple. I hadn't realized this existed. I can text Barb or Angie to get Lilly to come get me.*

Except that locked in here, her phone had no service. Head down, eyes focused on the reception bars on her phone, she walked down a ramp lined with stone walls that took her further into the bowels of the temple. From the outside of the temple, there was no indication that this back area even existed. *Oh well, might as well explore,* she thought. Naked light bulbs hung in a line, hanging low, an inch from her head. More light emanated from rooms off to each side. A room on the left was filled with piles of ceremonial supplies. Another room on the right was mostly empty except for some free-standing benches made with rope. Jaya walked into it, and plopped down on one of the benches, deciding to sit it out, as it wasn't likely anyone would hear her yelling for help. She noted the time and hoped that one of the many text messages she was trying to send would get through.

At least the priests will have to come back here, so someone will find me.

The minutes ticked away. The lack of stimulation after the sensory overload she had just experienced was nearly painful. Jaya cast her eyes around the room, at the bookshelves cut into the stone wall. Hopping off the bench and wincing from the pain in her rib, she wiggled a book out of a tightly packed shelf.

It was a book of hymns, made in a thick parchment, of the kind she had seen before. Jaya had to tug at the rough twine that bound the pages to see the contents, which crinkled like dried leaves as she manipulated them. She coughed. The pages were emitting a fine dust that was stifling the air. With nothing to do, she sat back down with the time-worn book in her hands. The pages were filled with handwritten Sanskrit script that she could sound out with concentration, but could not understand. She could read the Devanagari Hindi script, even if modern Hindi words were quite dissimilar from the original language.

An idea came to her. Josh was an ancient languages expert— she could ask him to translate. That would be cool, give them something to talk about next time they saw each other. It gave her a slight thrill to have found this book, maybe it was a family heirloom, seeing that it was housed in a temple on her family's land. Wouldn't it be vindicating to show Daadi Ma and her father? A sign of the value of coming here, that had nothing to do with finding a husband? The Panditji probably didn't even know this book existed. Satisfied with her plan, Jaya tucked the book into the waistband of her salwar pants and pulled the shirt, the kameez, over it.

Finally, after what felt like hours, she heard movement. The priests and a few members of their entourage were coming back down the hallway. Unsure of how to behave in this situation, Jaya nodded and smiled at them when they came face to face. She pantomimed to the older priests what had happened to her, that she had been pushed out of the temple and had found this area, but couldn't leave because the door was locked. She signaled to be let out and rushed back through the door when they did. If the priests seemed surprised, she was too far away to notice.

The temple was now mostly empty, and night had fallen. The air was much hotter and damper. Sounds came back to her ears in layers—first of insects, then of a low hum of talking and eating. She walked toward the light in the main hallway where she normally practiced yoga, where rows and rows of guests were seated on the floor, with leaf plates in front of them filled with food. Rushing up to Barb, who was mid-serve, she gave her an impulsive hug from behind.

"Jaya! Where were you?"

"Oh my God, Barb, I got locked in some random closet!"

"Yeesh! Are you okay?"

Jaya nodded. "Think so. What'd I miss? I'm so sorry. What do you guys need me to do? I feel *so* bad to have bailed on the work like this."

"No worries! We just looked up and you were gone! Just help me serve the rest of this, okay?" Barb transferred a big pot of lentils to Jaya, who grabbed it willingly and started ladling the meal out to guests who wanted second helpings.

Jaya breathed deeply to calm herself. As she watched the visitors of all walks of life eat their simple meals, she felt she was part of something bigger. She thought of how much fun she'd had in India so far. She'd met Barb and Angie at the ashram, Josh on the plane, Kabir and Ricki in Goa, and, of course, Silsilla and Banita and Banita's husband in Maalpur. And now she was at this awesome Shiva Moon Festival, hanging out with the world-famous Panditji who taught a world-renowned unique form of yoga. Her life had taken a turn she had not expected, and she couldn't have imagined how far she had come, both physically as well as spiritually. Looking at the big picture, her getting lost earlier was just no big deal.

Later, back in her room, Jaya got a call from Josh.

"Hey, Jaya," he said, loudly and excitedly.

"Yessss?" she replied, a bit loopy from the evening.

"So those pictures you texted. They were— It was amazing."

"Oh yeah, wasn't the festival beautiful? You should have seen the flowers, the colors and everything. I was just talking to the others about it."

"No, Jaya, not the festival. The book," he said insistently. "The pictures of the book. I translated what you sent; it's amazing."

"Oh. Really?" Jaya twirled her hair, smiling at the sound of his voice. "Yeah, it was something I found in the temple. I mean I figured since you're an expert, you could take a look."

"No, Jaya, I mean— I don't want to alarm you, but there is something, I don't know, odd about that book. Super odd. Not in a good way. We need to talk. I mean really talk."

"Huh? Why can't we just talk now? You're scaring me a bit," Jaya said, sitting down. Her stomach sank. He was acting like a drama queen. Was Josh going to turn out to be a nutjob?

"No, listen, I don't think it's a good idea for you to discuss this where you're at... in Maalpur or in the ashram. I don't— Listen, have you told anyone... about this book?"

"Just Barb and Angie, why?" Jaya said, getting defensive.

"But, okay, this is important. Did you tell the Panditji?"

"No, why? Josh, now you're scaring me!"

"Oh okay," he paused for a beat. The silence pounded right through her. "Jaya, you probably shouldn't have done that. Told anyone. But at least the Panditji doesn't know. It's important that he not know."

"If you say so. Come off it, Josh, what IS in that book?"

"Listen, I can tell you, but—"

"But what, Josh?"

"Can you come meet me in Delhi this weekend?"

"I mean, Josh, if you want to see me, just say so! There's no need for this drama," Jaya said, getting annoyed.

"No, Jaya, no, listen, I'm messing this up..." he trailed off, berating himself. "Listen, you need to come to Delhi so I can tell you about this book. You can't tell anyone else about it, okay? Promise me. And promise me, whatever you do, just bring the book with you, and do not under any circumstances tell the Panditji about it."

And he hung up, leaving Jaya listening to the dial tone until the operator came on to ask her in a high-pitched and blurry voice if she needed to make a call.

CHAPTER EIGHT

Book of Deeds

Josh was waiting for Jaya in the old part of Delhi, in a public park whose paths radiated geometrically from the center mausoleum of a long-dead Mughal emperor. The grass was soft and overused, tamped down by the enthusiasm of the locals enjoying its space—cricket players, picnickers, young lovers, and children. The mausoleum was, meanwhile, decaying. Its marble tiles that once formed a mosaic had long since fallen off, or been removed, and the walls now appeared to be made of spongy, graying stone. Pigeons took shelter in the hallways surrounding the mausoleum, nesting in the corners of the ceiling and leaving droppings on unsuspecting passersby.

"Hey you," Josh said, spying Jaya in jeans and light sandals, a weekend backpack carefully slung over her shoulder. She had come straight from the train station in an auto rickshaw.

"Hey back," Jaya said, seeing Josh in his tank top, looking out of place amongst the more conservatively dressed Indians. "Wow, Josh, drama much?"

Josh gave her a bear hug and kissed her cheek. "Yeah, uh, it's for a good reason. I swear. Did you bring the book?"

After Goa, the air between them was even more electric than before. Jaya noticed that she felt drawn to him and that she liked the feeling. She dug around in her backpack and produced the book. For safe-keeping, it was wrapped up in a plastic bag, to prevent spills from ruining it.

"Ta-da!" she sang, displaying the book as if she were on a TV commercial. "Here it is! I can't wait to show this thing to my family back home!"

"Here, let's just, let's just go over here," Josh said, suddenly nervous, leading her off the grass and into one of the many stone hallways.

They seated themselves under a large open window, which had been carved out of the wall to allow air flow.

"Could you please tell me, Josh, what is so incredibly important about this book that I had to travel all the way to Delhi? I mean, now I'm very curious."

Josh couldn't wait to tell Jaya what he had discovered. Ever since he'd translated the text, he had been obsessed. Here was a new research project, one that he hadn't even expected to do. With his own book languishing, he had thrown himself into studying the photos Jaya had sent over late nights and early mornings. What he found was unexpected. He had assumed to find pre-printed religious text, filled with passages of the Vedas. These texts were quite common in his research and had varied remarkably little over time. Rather, what Jaya had sent was a series of journal entries, written by hand in an arcane Sanskrit, which Josh had been able to discern with difficulty. Without a doubt, as Josh relayed to Jaya now, this was an amazing find. This journal, at least based on what she had shared with him, was over seven hundred years old.

As Jaya listened, her jaw dropped. "But this is unbelievable!" she exclaimed. "You're telling me this is something from my family's history, right? A journal of their past. What luck!"

"Actually, Jaya," Josh looked uncomfortable, "it's about the Panditji."

A feeling in the pit of her stomach took hold. She slumped closer to the ground. There had been too many odd moments with the Panditji. And her mind flashed back to Silsilla's warning.

"How is the Panditji involved?"

"That's the thing, Jaya. This book, well, it's more of a journal. More specifically, it's Panditji's journal. I'm convinced only he could have written it based on what you've told me about him."

Jaya looked down at the volume in her hands. How was it possible that this book had anything to do with the Panditji? She had found it on her family's grounds, tucked away in an area rarely accessed. And Panditji had only recently arrived, as Silsilla had said. It was discomforting, to experience one layer of time folding back upon another, to wonder if the truths that presented themselves as a crystal blue lake were, in fact, murky bog waters.

Josh reached out and caressed Jaya's cheek, to turn her face toward him. "Um, okay. Here goes," he took a deep breath, dramatically, "I swear to you now, Jaya, that what I'm showing you is the God's honest truth. You can tell me I'm wrong, you can blow me off and never talk to me again, and I get that you might do that. So." He took out a well-kept, scratch-free black spiral notebook from his backpack. "I used this to make notes as I translated. The first round for words, the second for meaning. You know this is what I do for work so.... Just ah, sit here and read it. It's quiet. No one will see, after all."

Entry 1:

Here now, I record my past as Hausa Maharaj, the head disciple of yogi Guru Hauka Maharaj, head acolyte to King Chandragupta the Third, of the glorious sun city of Dharmavapillai in the year 1320. I record here now the system of yoga that has been perfected, passed down to me by my guru.

This yogic system is made up of five elements—the mind, the breath, the body, the heart, the touch. In the mind, one must be fearless, to cut out the fears that drive most humans and keep us separated from the mortals. In the breath, one must always breathe deeply and slowly, a measured breath, so that each moment is the same, one after the last, even when exerting oneself. This is the secret to a long life, to not waste the breath but use it with thought. In the body, one must remain pliable and flexible, slim and strong. This is achieved through yogic poses. In the heart, one should be filled with duty and love. If the heart has feeling, then the life is always moving in the proper direction, toward God. In the touch, one should never deceive, and in our sexual relations, they should not be used for power but to achieve oneness. These principles I record here now.

Entry 2:

After some calamities involving my guru, it became necessary to choose another path. This new path was undertaken after a ritual performed by Sadhu Ram Dharan at the ghats of Varanasi. This gave control over my own death and eventual return, which is why I now have total control over my own reincarnation. With Sadhu Ram's blessings, I have gained true power over the cycle of life, and my yogic practice has been even more successful. I arranged also to have my faithful assistant and lover, Ravi Kumar, perform this ceremony, so we could be together through this journey of multiple lives. This recording shall serve witness and continuity should time and distance erase my memories.

"What is this?! Josh, are you kidding me with this?" Jaya said. She suppressed a violent shiver that started just under her neck and ended in a sneeze. Being witness to history was one thing, but this was something quite different.

"Do you see here, where the text says 'reincarnation'?" Josh said. "Well, I looked up that word in one of my Sanskrit books, because I couldn't figure out what it meant. You know, Sanskrit has evolved over time and because of that, at the publisher, we keep texts from multiple points in history, so that we can compare writing styles and meanings when we complete our translations. Anyway, I cross-referenced this word. It *does* mean reincarnation."

"But could you be mistaking the meaning?" Jaya asked cautiously, tugging on a lock of her hair in her confusion.

"I think you need to keep reading," Josh insisted gently.

Entry 3:

I have come full cycle. At an early age of this new life, the memories of my yogic system and past life returned. My guru's execution at the hands of his bitter rival, a new yogi who had gained the King Chandragupta's attention. Escaping to Varanasi. My choice of a new path and death on the Varanasi ghats at the hands of Sadhu Ram Dharan. My return to the yoga ashram which I had established under Chandragupta's rule, now part of a new village called Maalpur. The new Kings rule now here, from the South. Recognizing the ashram immediately, I knew that this was the right path. With my past yogic knowledge, I quickly gained authority as the master yogi over the place. And when it was possible, I went to a hiding place off the main temple, and I began to write this record. I am recording this account now at fifty years of age. It has been a strange kind of life, with my superior knowledge of the human condition I have gained power quickly, but not affection. My dear Ravi is lost to me throughout time. I have sought him. I have sought him in others. It is of no use.

"Maalpur," Jaya breathed. "This all happened there? That little town my dad's family is from? Where I was just hanging out? And this supposed ritual to master reincarnation actually worked? How is this even possible?"

Josh was staring patiently at Jaya now. He grabbed her hand, clasping her fingers in his. Looking into her eyes, he asked, "Are you not at all curious to guess who might be the master yogi?"

"The Panditji," she said with absolute certainty, squeezing his hand for strength. "He wasn't lying," she murmured, "about this being his land. The Panditji, he wasn't lying." She recalled with regret her arrogant surety that the Panditji was embellishing his connection to her family's land, in order to snooker dumb foreigners out of their money with his supposedly "ancient" system of yoga. Or how her own Daadi Ma believed that the Panditji was a recent transplant to the land. *How wrong we've been*, she thought. *He'd been telling the truth about it all.*

"No, he wasn't lying. He was telling the truth," Josh said out loud what she was thinking, fidgeting with his hair. "His age, though, is the big lie. Did he tell you he was in his fifties? Because he's not, Jaya. If the first entry in this journal is correct, then he's been alive for, oh, let's say, at least seven hundred years."

Asked about this moment much later in life, Jaya always described the silence and the lack of air around her and how her world went entirely still. The flies stopped buzzing. The cars stopped honking. The kids stopped screaming. In this moment, she was pushed into total sensory deprivation, in this tomblike structure, with the book in her hands. She was remembering the Panditji's oily, dark eyes upon her in the yoga hall. All knowing. All seeing. A deep shiver ran through her. Of course. Of course.

A Mexican restaurant in the central part of town was the escape they needed to get away from the dark secrets of the past; they immersed themselves in the corn-rich, tequila-soaked meal while jerky Hindi pop music blared. Agreeing that it couldn't get any crazier than this, Josh ordered two lemon drop shots, which he claimed tasted better due to the indigenous Indian lemon-lime, and the limey sweet vodka loosened them both up. Ignoring the fact that they were in public, he leaned over the table and kissed her as the shot glasses hit the table, empty.

"You'd better let me hold onto this book, Jaya," Josh said, caressing her shoulder. "So I can translate the rest of it. Who knows what other deep, dark secrets lurk in the Panditji's diary?"

Wordlessly, Jaya found the book in her backpack and handed it over. She was feeling a bit grungy after her long train journey, the afternoon in the park, and now the smoky restaurant. But also alive, she realized. What an adventure this was all turning out to be. Who would have thought the Panditji would have such a secret? It tickled her that she was connected to this. She chuckled to herself, imagining Daadi Ma ambling over to the stove to make her morning cup of tea right now, blissfully unaware of the chain of events she had set off.

"What's got you smiling?" Josh asked. "I'm probably not going to be sleeping for the next three days while I translate the rest of this *insane* diary. So spare a smile for me, while you're resting on your train ride back to Maalpur."

Josh closed his notebook with a flourish, just as a boisterous after-work crew at the next table spilled a drink.

"Should we get out of here?" Jaya asked.

In companionable silence, they rose and paid the bill, exiting the third-floor restaurant via an elevator down to the street. Arm in arm, they made their way back to Josh's apartment.

The next morning, after Jaya had fallen asleep on Josh's rattan couch, they were eating leftover burritos. There wasn't much time left for her to shower and get back on the overnight train.

"So, are you going to ask him?" Josh asked her.

"Ask who what?"

"Are you going to ask the Panditji, you know, about his reincarnation? I think you should. What a story that would be!"

"Haven't decided," Jaya said. "He's a control freak, and he seems super concerned about appearances, so I'd rather not discuss it with him. Maybe it could be a deep, dark family secret."

Jaya's train journey was different this time. On her way to Maal-pur the first time, she had desperately hoped that she would be liked and accepted by the yogi, by her fellow yoga practitioners, by everyone really, and in that rush, she saw only the good. She had soaked in the romantic nature of the countryside, the mushy green grass, the low red-brick walls, the cows grazing. She was dazzled. But now, she knew more. Now she knew that what looked solid and what she knew to be fact could be built on layers of lies. And so, she began to question her surround-ings.

She saw only the dilapidation of the buildings and the an-tiquity of farming life. Why, she saw men riding donkey carts and tilling the soil with oxen, as their ancestors must have done in the past. It wasn't surprising that this place could harbor the Panditji for seven hundred years. She realized she was sur-rounded by the creeping backwardness of an old place with an old people. And the only reason they had not moved forward, held in check for centuries, was because of corruption and raw poverty, masked in religion to hide all manner of sins.

Josh stayed up all night after Jaya left, using the book to complete his translations. With the first pot of coffee brewed, he dived into the next section.

Entry 4:

It is 1550, and in the years between my natural death and my return, the old Kings are gone and there are new Kings, Muslims from the North. I am highly sought after by these new Kings, by the sadhus, by the rich householders. All seek to be around me, because I know the old ways that they want, that they believe will restore their former glory. They have showered the ashram with tributes; Ravi and I live comfortable lives, with the best clothing, the finest jewels, the richest house, the best trained household staff. In me there is a growing anger and little patience for humans. With just the one life that is unplanned and abrupt, they are no better than animals. Their pains, their fears, their joys are all out of their control. But I am in control. That is why, when another yogi from Haridwar came to visit, with claims to have a new, purer yogic technique, I listened, and I observed. But as I told him, as he lay foaming at the mouth with the poison that my dearest Ravi had so lovingly poured for him, there was no way this could be the case, as he had been alive only one life, and one life was nowhere near long enough to know the deepest mysteries of life. To the seeker of truth and beauty, only the one with the purest soul, the truest and most accurate eye, free from distraction of all human markings, can hold sway.

Josh gasped, jolting his coffee cup and failing to stop drops from hitting his off-white couch. A rock dropped straight to the bottom of his stomach.

"Poison?" he muttered to himself. "Shit, shit!" He immediately texted Jaya to ask her to call him as soon as she woke up. Nervous now and unable to do anything to help her, he flipped his notebook and decided to get the rest of this translated as soon as possible. With any luck, he could complete the work before Jaya arrived in Maalpur. Based on Josh's calculations, the next section appeared to have been written in the late 1600s. He still had eons to get through.

Entry 5:
Trading is the new religion. The ashram has new patrons, merchants who give gold to us to keep the traditions of yoga alive and to teach their sons. Our yoga system is now much established, and

we are the keepers of this. A banker in the main town, of the Patak family, is now storing my gold, would that it holds through to the next life. I have become wise to the ways of men—they stay always the same.

Entry 6:

It is 1686, and the ashram has been made into living quarters for visiting people of importance. I was for years unable to return to the ashram due to many impediments. Finally, after much work I have been able to access my book, my temple, my ashram. I regret that the manner of doing so required committing someone to their death—the laws of men cannot hold me after all.

Entry 7:

The Kingdom is now a part of a much larger principality, and the Kings are great patrons of the arts and all the old ways, and I am in much demand. The ashram and the temple have been rebuilt into even finer glory. I have much comfort in this life, retrieving my gold, finding Ravi.

Entry 8:

It is 1830, and the English people are now in control of this area. The farmers seek patronage, and the old kings are mostly diminished or gone. I have established the ashram as a kind of religious center. The Englishmen leave us be, content to keep the populace happy whilst they seek the jewels and spices that drew their sights here in the first place. The banking family, the Pataks, have misplaced my gold. I am left penniless, but it is no matter. With our system of yoga, we are greatly revered by these new rulers, who allow us to keep our land undisturbed and ask for no tax nor custom in return.

Entry 9:

The Englishmen have brought nothing but corruption; they are leeches upon our land. The local men have been conscripted to fight wars on soils far from ours. Unable to farm, the fields lie unturned, and our crops suffer, and the farmers starve. The riches and glories of our past seem long past. Ravi and I have started an annual moon festival to honor Shiva, in order to remember, in order to celebrate our culture. It is an important thing that we can do, and it keeps the people happy, and on our side. I remember, as does Ravi, and we fill the nights with stories of our past, which others come to hear of, from far and wide. One must be careful though. Recently an elderly farmer came, someone whom I recognized from a previous life. He looked at me very strangely when I told these stories, and said he remembered them, told almost exactly the same way, from when he was a boy. It will not do to be too careful, in this new age. People live longer now, and it seems some may remember me, as I was from before.

It was already dawn when Josh came upon the last section. As with most mornings in Delhi, the day started humid and foggy. The lone cries of milk sellers with their buffaloes, walking up and down his residential block, were the only sounds. He couldn't help but be fascinated by what he was reading. The Panditji had lived for so many years, seen so much. It was clear that he wasn't totally human anymore. To think that Josh had stumbled upon this, as a result of meeting this fascinating woman, was beyond his comprehension. "Jaya," he said to himself. He stood up, too quickly, then sat back down again. It was still early. Her train wouldn't have arrived yet. He needed, he decided, to finish translating this chapter immediately, so he could give her the full picture of the danger she might be in. He would have to tell her that she was returning to Maalpur into the clutches of a murderer—a debased, thoroughly corrupt man—who by dint of his long, long life had been able to outsmart legions of suspecting rivals and enemies. He gulped down his coffee and pushed himself to read faster.

Entry 10:
It all moves faster now—power can move across distance. Voice can move across distance. Images and sound move across distance. Even history. Now even stories can move across distance. There are fewer secrets now. The Englishmen are gone. The ashram has been given to a prosperous family and is much changed. There is electricity, and parts have been shored up with new materials. Still, I established a foothold there and have continued my practice, with people coming from many places, all these countries, clamoring for the ancient ways and the discipline. Ravi came to me later in life. We marvel in the degradation of humanity; in the lack of discipline in the mind and body, which seems to permeate the human condition. Thankfully, we are no longer human. We are avatars, copies of earlier men, harder, deeper than what exists today. I am the living embodiment of the atman, the spirit of the universe, through which all strains of time—past, present, and future—collide.

When Jaya arrived in Maalpur, after expertly timing her jump onto the platform from the slowing train, with her backpack in tow, she got caught up in a commotion. A man had been accused of stealing from the newspaper vendor, and the station police had arrived to apprehend the culprit. The man, a rather robust man with longish hair, broke free of the police, and as he fled, he ran into Jaya. She spun around and fell flat on the ground. Passersby rushed to lift her up by her shoulders and ask her if she was okay. "Yes, yes," she said hurriedly. When she touched an ache in her arm, she discovered he'd stolen her back-pack. By the time she told the police, it was too late to catch the thief. He was probably out in the fields, leaving Jaya with only her small purse, her phone and wallet. *At least I had carried these separately*, she thought. *At least Josh had the book, thank goodness.* The rest was replaceable.

Declining to file a police report, Jaya sunk into the back of a taxi, a late-model Ambassador, mint green in color, and turned on her phone. The driver was an older gentleman with white hair and acne scars on his face. He nodded at her and started the car's ignition; 50s-era Hindi music came on. Then the cab lurched out of the parking lot and took a left onto the main street. Jaya watched the town go by, then observed as the car took a right at a juncture where signs clearly pointed the other way for Maalpur. Before she could say anything, she gasped at the barrage of text messages on her phone. They were all from Josh.

"Josh," she said urgently, after she had called and he had picked up on the first ring. "What. What is it?'

"Jaya, where are you?"

"Maalpur."

"Listen to me very carefully. Go to a police station. Somewhere safe. Jaya, Panditji is more than what you think. He and Ravi, they are murderers, Jaya. They've killed people. With poison."

"What!?" Jaya said. She closed her eyes in fear, wishing she could be anywhere but here. The fields around her looked never-ending, she was quite literally in the middle of this vast country, away from everything she knew. Panicking, she tried to take deep breaths. She had never felt fear like this before.

"Excuse me, isn't Maalpur supposed to be the other way?" Jaya nervously asked the driver.

"Ma'am, actually I was told you should be dropped here," the driver replied.

A text message arrived.

> It's Ravi. Know u have book. Bring back, NOW.
> PKM very very angry!

Jaya closed her eyes again, sinking into the car seat. She was in a pickle now, alone, and going who-knows-where. She was truly scared. This was all too real.

By now they had left town and were on a wide highway, where stone road markers sat on either side and large trees with leafy branches stretched over the road, forming a natural arch. In an earlier, simpler time, these trees and markers may have been ways to channel drivers. Now they were death traps, hazards to speeding cars trying to pass one another. The taxi came upon a clearing, and the asphalt quickly turned to flattened mud. There were low walls dividing the plots of land into squares as far as the eye could see.

They drove on the dirt road for almost twenty minutes before arriving at a mud hut with straw thatching.

"Here? Surely, you cannot be serious," Jaya said.

"Ma'am, this is where they said to meet you."

"They? Who is *they*?" Jaya asked, incredulously.

"Please do not worry, just be here, come inside," the driver said.

It seemed Jaya would have no choice but to get out. As she approached the hut, she noticed an elderly man outside lounging on a traditional charpoy cot made of thick handwoven rope. He wore a large red turban, the sort that farmers sometimes wore, and a dhoti, a long cloth wrapped around his waist and legs. He was smoking a thin cigarette, and his eyes were bloodshot, his hands long and gnarled, his skin dark from the sun. The man of indeterminate age stood up and bowed in greeting. She nodded at him, and he motioned that she should come inside.

Miles from anything and unclear whom she would meet inside—and afraid to even guess—Jaya had no choice. She stepped over the bottom of the metal door frame and ducked her head to avoid hitting the low ceiling. Once inside and out of the sun, she found the room cooler and larger than it looked from the outside, with its cement floors and high windows letting in the light. The air was smoky and dusty—but also stale. The driver, who stepped in after her, pulled out a chair from a table and asked her to sit. She sat. The turbaned man entered with a glass of water, which she took gratefully and downed in one gulp. It was cool, lemony, and minty.

The man stepped backwards and joined his palms in a pranam bow. He followed the driver out and pulled the door shut. The clanking of a padlock and heavy chain being locked came soon after. She couldn't see out the high windows, but it wouldn't have mattered anyway, because Jaya's eyes had inexplicably stopped seeing. That was her last thought as she slumped in her chair, falling sideways onto the floor. She landed hard on her elbow. The thud momentarily woke her up enough to make the connection: she'd been drugged.

CHAPTER NINE

The Pollution

Reality returned to Jaya in flashes. She felt the insistent movement of a vehicle, its lurching stops, its tires rotating with effort on grooved, gravel roads. Next, her vision. She perceived, more than saw, bright lights but could not focus, as if a thick lotion had gummed up her eyes and lids and lashes. A few moments later, she felt a pounding in her head and began to understand that she was staring at a car door, at a black door latch, the kind that pushed down. She remembered the train station and the taxi that had taken her to the hut in the middle of nowhere. She remembered being locked in the hut and hitting the floor. Drugged. She must have been drugged. To calm herself, she moved to swipe her hair out of her face and found that she could not. Looking down, she was surprised to see her hands bound with a dingy white rag. A sharp sting in her elbow spread all the way to her neck, and she fell back against the scratchy car seat. Blind panic coursed through her, hot and edgy and shrill, an electric current. Tied and deeply uncomfortable, she could only close her eyes and try to bring herself into the present, into what was happening here, in the reality that she was in now.

It had not been not easy for Josh to find the phone number to the Maalpur police station. When he had and called it, they knew nothing about Jaya's whereabouts.

"Are you sure, sir, that you are looking for someone in Maalpur itself?" the dispatcher had asked. "Right now, there is not anyone of this description here."

"No, no," Josh said, feeling helpless, "that's the point. Someone has kidnapped her. I think, someone from the big ashram, the PKM Ashram."

"Ashram? The holy place. Sir, surely, you must be mistaken. Kindly please check your missing person's cellphone location, and then call us back if you truly have an issue."

At first, Josh tried to rationalize. Jaya's phone battery was dead. She was out of cellphone range. She was busy and wasn't picking up his calls. But as the hours ticked by, he feared the worse. And the police didn't seem willing to help. In desperation, he'd called upon Amrita. She was always the first to insert herself into any ongoing dispute or question in their office. Maybe she could help on this, too.

"My friend is missing," he'd texted her. "What should I do?"

"Where has ur friend gone lost? Delhi?" Amrita texted back, almost instantaneously.

"No, in a small town, Maalpur."

"Where? Then immediately call someone u know there, or then go there urself. The police no help," she replied.

That triggered an idea. Josh went to Jaya's social media page to find MJ, who contacted Jaya's mother, who was imperious at first, a defense against her doubts about this Josh character whose voice she was hearing for the first time.

"You really cannot blame me," she said to Josh with some anger, her voice shaking with overexcitement. "I don't even know you! How do you know my daughter? And now you say she is missing? From the ashram? This is all very fantastical. You'll forgive me, if I think you might just be pranking me, or up to some other mischief."

Josh steeled himself and answered Kiran patiently. No, she did not know him. Yes, she could trust him. No, he had no reason to wish ill of her daughter. They had met on the plane. There seemed to be something untrustworthy about the ashram and its Panditji. "As far as I can tell, Mrs. Gupta, she seems to have disappeared upon returning to Maalpur," he said, with polite contrition.

Kiran sighed. "So," she said, twirling her gold bangle while speaking, knowing that she had no choice but to deal with the situation, "let me call Silsilla Auntie, my mother-in-law's friend and see. You don't go anywhere, okay?"

For two hours, Josh sat by the phone, heart racing, becoming increasingly agitated. He wavered between making reservations for the next train to Maalpur and taking his publisher's van (and driver) to hightail it and find her. He also wondered if he should call the police again, despite Amrita's advice, or start an all-out social media push to find Jaya.

Kiran's return call did not help. "Silsilla Auntie does not know where Jaya is. She called the ashram and has been rebuffed. She is sending her driver to look for her now. Josh, what the hell is going on?"

"Mrs. Gupta," he said slowly, gripping the phone has tightly as he could, as if doing so would make the connection better, "you don't know me. You have no reason to believe me. And I don't know how exactly to say this. We found out that the ashram, well, I know it's on your family's land, but... How to say this—"

"Just say it!" Daadi Ma yelled into Kiran's speakerphone. "Hi, Josh, this is Jaya's Daadi Ma, her grandmother. Now, my granddaughter is missing. After all, what IS it? You young people these days are so dramatic!"

"The Panditji, Mrs. Gupta, the one who is at the ashram. He's not normal. He has secrets, I guess is the way to say it. And we think," he gulped, feeling guilty, "we think he knows that Jaya knows about his, well, his secret. Well, that is, we were hoping he didn't know that Jaya knew, but because she's missing, we have to assume that maybe he does."

"What secret? Hai Ram," Daadi Ma said, calling out to the gods.

"Do not try to move. We will be there soon," a voice said from the front of the car.

Confusion mixed with alarm. Jaya thought she saw a face, but she could not tell whose. She slumped back in the seat, and closed her eyes again. The car's movement slowed, then stopped. The sensation made her insides churn, and she twisted to her side, all of a sudden becoming violently sick. Miserable, with a sour taste in her mouth, she couldn't help the vomit from dribbling down her chin, throat, and blouse, to the tops of her pants. She could not even wipe it off with her hands. Then came the awkward realization that she would have to angle herself to nudge her shoulder up and clean her face. Jaya's whole body shivered, as she began to understand the enormity of her situation. *Trapped. I'm trapped.*

At that moment, the door hinged open, and two men pulled her out and propped her upright, her feet still unsteady. Her eyes rebelled against the brightness of the sunlight. She felt like wilting in place and falling asleep for eternity. Instead, she was forced to walk into what hazily appeared to be the ashram. Her mind uncontrollably flashed back to the Panditji's face—his charismatic smile, his all-knowing eyes—and all that she had learned about him. His big secret about his reincarnation and now, apparently, his murders. Every single atom in her body wished to resist what might come next. She was pushed through a door underground, then she tripped and hopped down a poorly lit, bumpy stone walkway. The men then shoved her into a side room. *I'm being taken to the back area of the temple, where I got lost before*, she thought, and held onto that knowledge as she resolved to observe her situation fully, as her only weapon against what might come next.

Narrow and dark, the room she was in was made of stone, with hard benches cut into each wall, as if the entire room had been carved out of a massive boulder. It was lit by a series of small lamps. Her eyes, still adjusting, had trouble focusing on any one thing. She hardly noticed as the men pushed her to sit on one of the benches. Fear had overtaken her, and the adrenalin brought on by the fight-or-flight response pumped through her. Would it all be over now? She wondered what she would do, as she focused on Ravi's form entering the room, wishing she had never even returned to Maalpur. What had she been thinking?

"Don't talk. Sssh..." Ravi whispered. She looked down and saw with some detachment that he was freeing her bound hands. She opened her jaw to unlock it. Tried to swallow but her throat was sore. She closed her eyes and tried to breathe. These were all attempts on her part to focus on the physical and to manage her rising terror. But she couldn't control that emotion. Thoughts about the depths of evil came screaming up and out of her like a geyser, in dramatic whooshes. The book. Josh's translation. The Panditji. Ravi. Their lives. Their crimes. Here she was, face to face with a man who had been continuously conscious for over seven hundred years, on his home turf. She did not know whether she was staring at a real human being or some other living thing that occupied a different place in the pantheon of consciousness.

"Drink please, you must having to be thirsty," Ravi insisted, smiling, handing her a stainless-steel cup of warm milk from a tray, behaving still as the courteous assistant despite Jaya's terrified expression.

She closed her eyes and muttered a prayer as she wordlessly gripped the cup in her hand. She remembered enough now, from the book that Joshua had translated, to know the drink was likely laced with poison. Would these be her last moments? Would she have the wits to survive? Her mind cast about desperately, for ways to escape. But she could not envision any. Her only shot at survival was to avoid drinking this cup of milk. This she knew for certain, down to the depths of her soul.

Concentrating on her core, she took a deep yogic breath to calm herself, as the Panditji had taught in those first few weeks of class. Ironic, that his teachings might be a comfort to her now. She recalled his words. "The breath is sacred," he had said, smiling beatifically, "and cleansing. Correct breath, taken in correct manner, will fill the body and the mind with positive energy."

So Jaya took the deepest breath possible, trying to calm her nerves. It was not a moment for passivity—she would have to take some action if she hoped to survive. Jaya had learned only recently, in reading the Panditji's diaries, that fate could be tampered with. A misbelief in a positive fate was a human condition she did not seek to perpetuate. But what to do? She pictured Daadi Ma in this situation. Daadi Ma, her hair out of its bun, her white sari fouled with vomit, her life threatened. If Jaya had to guess, she would bet that Daadi Ma would find a way to play helpless, employing a stalling tactic that would put the onus on the other party to expend more energy and give up. Which reminded her: Daadi Mai had also insisted on her taking cardamom on for nausea. Didn't she still have the shells sitting in her pocket? Jaya swallowed her fear and looked straight at Ravi.

"I can't," Jaya croaked, channeling Daadi Ma, "drink... just yet... my throat..." and she made a confused face, shrugged, and let her hands go limp, which caused the cup to tumble out of her hands and go clanging onto the stone floor. As the glass fell, she reached into her pocket and tossed five cardamom pods into her mouth, giving them a good chew and then squirreling them away to the sides of her cheek.

Wordlessly and gracefully, Ravi bent down to pick up the cup, succeeding in keeping most of the milk inside. He now stood up, and looming over her, he grabbed her jaw by one hand and attempted to pour the milk down her throat. His grip was strong. Her chin and lower jaw hurt. Jaya squeezed her lips and eyes shut, willing him to give up. Ravi thrust her down, and she felt her head slam into stone. Pain, shock, dizziness collided. He now pried open her mouth and poured the milk in. Jaya's body, her consciousness somewhere deep inside, now took over. Her gag reflex kicked in, and she started choking as the chewed cardamom husks hit the back of her throat, getting stuck. Between the sour smell of the poisoned milk and the cardamom pods, Jaya's nausea rose, and she ended up vomiting everything that Ravi had tried to feed her. Feeling terrible, she closed her eyes, praying that perhaps she would survive.

When she next woke, who-knows-how-long later, the Panditji was staring down at her. He looked pure evil now. Dispassionately, she observed the creases and the wrinkles in his face, the falseness of his dyed hair, the moral emptiness in his eyes. Revolted by the sight of him, she felt bile rise in her throat, burning the back of it as all the milk that had been forced down her esophagus came rushing out. Jaya spit and choked, rolling to her side. She was beyond caring anymore. And something in the Panditji's countenance made her want to fight.

"So, Jaya, such a difficult girl who has come to my ashram," he said now. The Panditji's voice boomed. She had never heard his voice so loud before; he sounded far different from the urbane man leading the yoga classes. "You are a guest at my choosing, but you have violated my hospitality," he continued sharply, "and you have something that belongs to me."

"I'm not a guest on your land, and you know it. This place is just as much my family's as it is yours."

"You'll give the book back," the Panditji said firmly.

"I don't have it with me. Maybe if you release me, I can get it to you."

"Perhaps," he said, noncommittally.

"How did you do it, Panditji? How did you convince all these people that you were someone worth following, hiding such a big secret?" Jaya taunted.

"Oh ho, so you think that you know about my secrets, do you? No, I don't think you really know. No, I don't think you do. The diary, you translated it, I presume?" he asked, not waiting for an answer. "Well, that diary is only going to tell you so much. And since you asked, perhaps I will tell you, about my secrets. While we wait."

"Wait? For what?" Jaya asked.

"For the poison, dear girl, the one that Ravi fed you, to work. I'll quite enjoy watching you slip away. Your grandmother was so very insistent that I accept you here, do you know? I wonder if she'll feel the same in a few days, when she hears about this. But don't worry, my dear, it will be a good sort of life-leaving for you. And in fact, it will be better, you see? Because yoga cannot be fully achieved until you leave this mortal situation you are in. So just listen to your teacher now. Just let yourself drift away. I'll tell you a story, to keep you company, and you can close your eyes, there you go, and go to sleep and ignore any pains and fears."

Jaya closed her eyes, unwilling to accept the Panditji's soothing voice into her mind. Bits of milk and spit dribbled out of her mouth. Hyper vigilant of any potential sign that the poison was working, she thought of her family, of course, but also to her surprise, of Josh. She loved how sweet he was, and how enthusiastic, and how he'd made time to meet her in Goa and helped her translate the book. It was a shame that perhaps what they had would never get to see a future. She hoped he wouldn't be too upset when he found out that he hadn't been able to help her. She tried to close her eyes and imagine a life with Josh, one where they dated and moved back to New York, got married even. At least she could dream. Anything, she thought, to distract herself from what the Panditji was saying.

Imperiously, like a conquering king, he spoke.

"My life began in the year 1292. Then, I was born Vikram Gupta. My parents were an important family in this area. We spent much time at the king's palace, and when I was of a young age, my parents made me a disciple to the yoga master. Guru Hauka Maharaj, my guru, had a very unique style of Purushutara yoga, which you also are learning. That was where I learned my technique, you see. King Chandragupta, who we served, was very pleased, and we were given the best. All the fineries and the jewels. Then, a bad king, from the south, came to Dharmavapillai, that is Maalpur's ancient name, to steal our land. Our land, Jaya. Not your family's. No, never your family's land. It has always been mine. Yes, the southern king and his henchmen murdered our king—very quickly. Then they came for the ashram, and my noble guru, he also was killed. I lived only due to escape—Ravi and I ran away from the Kingdom in the night, while Guruji was being murdered, to flee to Varanasi."

Panditji paused briefly.

Miraculously, despite feeling panic from head to toe, Jaya could discern no change in her physical state. A spark of hope pulsed inside her. With a calm she did not know she could muster, she began to work through the possibilities of escaping. Her mind moved quickly. It looked like there was only one way out of this room: through the door that the Panditji was currently sitting in front of. There was no other option. The benches were carved of stone. The walls were stone. The floors were stone, too, and caked with a hardened, waxy film from years of candle-burning. There was a small six-inch grate in the floor for drainage. But beyond the drain and the door, there was not a single opening in this stone enclosure out of which to flee. The only light came from the candles placed every few inches along the walls. They burned in small pools of oil. Any kerfuffle could lead to fire, lit instantly by flame and the greasy, buttery floor. Panditji sighed, adjusted his dhoti crease, and continued.

"As I was saying, Varanasi when I arrived was full of life. It was the center of the world. On the streets were all the most dedicated gurus and swamis and holy men. On the banks of the Ganges River, on the ghats, I began yoga again, taking in many new students. But desire for what was lost, the wealth, the jewels, the luxury, filled me. I was angry, you see, very angry. I am thinking I should not have done it. But you see, Jaya, this is the weakness of man. The sadhu, he told us he could give us control over the wheel of life, the chakra, over life and death. Here was power, you see, in a very raw form. His name was Sadhu Ram Dharan, he was filthy and old, and many said a fake sadhu. A crazy old man. It did not matter. My mind was clear. I said yes. The day of my death arrived, as I knew it would. I was sick with fever. In those days, there was no recovery. You will see very soon, Jaya, death is not to be feared. The sadhu performed a ritual over my shivering body. This would grant me the powers to hold my consciousness across lives. I begged Ravi also to come

with me, and he agreed. But Ravi was a healthy young man. So, we watched as Ravi plunged a dagger into his very own stomach and then as he was bleeding, the priest performed the same ritual. Now you see, we are on the wheel. Death. Birth. Death. Birth."

Panditji circled the air with his finger, mimicking a cycle to emphasize his point, looking absently at Jaya.

"You see, nirvana, liberation, moksha, heaven as you modern people will call it, it never came. So, I follow no laws of man— only laws of nature. Men are weak and soft. Nature is hard, vicious, powerful. This is the learning."

The sound of a rolling cart came to her ears now. Squeaking and shifting, it rumbled on the stone floor. She shifted her body imperceptibly to the left, so she could open one eye and see what was happening.

"Move the body, Ravi, to the area with the others," the Panditji said, commandingly.

"Yes, of course, my dear," Ravi replied. "I'll be right on it. You go, rest now. Prepare yourself, for the evening."

A cold realization washed through Jaya as she lay there. She *was* "the body". They thought she was dead. But then she also realized something else. *The poison must not have worked.* After all, her body was still warm and breathing, and she had a pulse, and her cheeks were probably still flush. She understood now that she would be compelled to take action. There was no other option. From her field of vision lying on the bench, she could see only one set of legs: those of Ravi's, busying himself with the cart. His back was to her, and he was about six feet away. He was placing a cloth sheet on the cart, presumably a shroud in preparation to wrap her corpse up.

Summoning the strength she had left, she rolled herself sideways, quietly, and cautiously moved herself into a seated position, putting one foot, then the other, gently on the stone floor. A brisk, cold sensation shot up her feet and caused her legs to tingle. This was no time for fear, she told herself sternly, forcing herself to stand, crouch, and shuffle silently toward the door. Her heart pulsed inside her body. Steadily, she willed herself to move forward, creeping past Ravi's form, still turned away from her.

As she neared the door's entrance, Jaya froze as Ravi noticed in his periphery that something was askance. He did a double take, then reached out and weakly grabbed for her. But Jaya was too quick. With an agility born of three months of yoga and a spurt of adrenalin, she feinted left and pushed herself out the doorway in a full sprint. She did not know where she was going, so she blindly ran up a stone ramp, heading toward more light, which she hoped would lead her outside. Ravi was behind her. Her knees burned. Her chest hurt. Her mind was flooded with the thought that it would be so easy to give up, to let go, to give in. In that moment, she imagined what her death would be like. Dark, painful, lonely. No one would know where she had died, or how. No one would know who she had been. She thought of what was waiting for her if she succeeded: Daadi Ma, her parents, MJ, Barb, Angie, Josh, happiness, the future. And so, it turned out, that was how her courage crested, like a wave, over the momentary desire to let go. Again, she was ready to fight.

Closing in behind her, Ravi grasped the bottom of her shirt, and she momentarily stumbled backwards. Her shirt ripped as she pulled away with all her might. Back exposed, the front of her shirt hanging in tatters, Jaya glanced back to see Ravi fall backwards onto the ground from the momentum. Turning, she ran straight ahead, her arms clutching her front in modesty.

"Run, Jaya, run" came the encouragement inside her. Daadi Ma's face appeared, swimming in front of her. She exhaled loudly and tried to remember the way she'd been brought in. There was a door, up ahead. She found it, unsuccessfully pulling the heavy steel, then pushing forward. As she did, she caught a glimpse of Ravi's form rising up again, giving chase. The metal door finally creaked open, and she slipped through.

The night air enveloped her immediately. The door opened out into the back entrance to the temple. Picking up speed, Jaya ran, her shaky legs finding their way across the bumpy, grassy field. It was pitch-black, and she took full advantage of this as she headed for what looked like flickering tealights near a black iron gate. She could hear Ravi's voice in the distance, sounding the alarm, then a guard dog's barking, then more shouting as others began to rouse. Rounding herself out the gate, Jaya continued to run and walk, fast as she could, for what seemed like miles.

Jaya knew where she was now; the central part of town was up ahead. Because it was night, the streets were emptier, and the journey she'd previously taken in an auto rickshaw didn't seem as far. She stayed in the shadows, near the ditches, and off to the side, so that she could avoid being noticed. Covered in vomit and spit, exhausted and crying, she felt unglued. Too keyed up to be hungry, she kept walking briskly, hour after hour.

As the night wore on, her fear settled and another sort of dull reality took its place. She had not been followed or found by the Panditji's people. She had survived, at least for now. At some point, she found herself sitting down on the ground and resting—just for a little while. But instead, she fell asleep in a heap. Nothing mattered anymore, and she was too tired to do anything more.

CHAPTER TEN

Tracks in the Old City

ours later, as the sun began its daily routine, Jaya was sitting in Silsilla's house in the little living room with the blue whitewashed walls, drinking a lemon fizzy water with salt. She had taken a long hot bath and had put on a nightgown and robe. Her hair was wet and brushed, her face fresh, and her stomach starting to feel the slightest bit hungry. Jaya felt like a survivor. It was a feeling she had never experienced before. She had managed to walk all the way to Silsilla's house during the long night, looking for road signs that led to the central district, where she found the movie theater—and the peach-colored house. Bone tired, she had collapsed and fallen asleep outside the gate, too exhausted to wake anyone and answer a barrage of questions at such an early hour. Silsilla's driver had been the one to find her, to his astonishment, when he had returned from his search for the American friend's granddaughter, this very person sleeping outside his madam's house.

Jaya's mind felt sharper, clearer this morning. Some intuition told her that she must limit what she told her hosts, and so despite their many attempts to understand who had taken her and how, she stuck to a barely believable story about the Panditji having some bad elements in his ashram, a taxi driver kidnapping her, and her escape. Begging off any more explanations and refusing to report the incident to the police, she agreed to a doctor's checkup the next morning and tucked into her breakfast of toast with butter, bean sprouts and a banana.

When Josh called as she was finishing her meal, Jaya slipped away into the guest room and told him everything.

"I told you the Panditji is a dangerous man!" Josh shouted into the phone, louder than necessary. He'd been up all night in his apartment, keyed up, unable to sleep and thinking. He cleared his throat apologetically and said, "I mean, do you really think he will let you go now, after you escaped? Knowing what you know? After he's already tried to poison you? I think he's going to come after you."

Alarm shot through Jaya's stomach and coursed to every nerve ending. She closed her eyes, unable to put up with any more fear.

"Josh, honestly, I mean this is small-town India here in Maalpur. The farthest he might go to find me is Delhi. I could fly home to New York!"

"Didn't you say his yoga students are all over the world? All it would take is for him to ask one of them to look you up. In New York or Maalpur or Delhi, wherever—does it really matter where? Do you want to live your life that way, looking around suspiciously and questioning everyone you meet?"

There was a pause. Jaya contemplated her next statement. While she wanted dearly for this all to go away, for this to be a surreal, but ephemeral, nightmare, she could not do that. And anyway, all this had introduced her to Josh, so she had to thank the cosmos for *something*.

"Project plans," Jaya said, cryptically.

"Huh?"

"Project plans, Josh. That's what I do, at work. You know, before I became this amazing person going to yoga ashrams and Goa with strangers I met on the plane."

"Very funny," Josh said. He was smiling, despite his fear for her.

"Let's think of the Panditji's life as a project plan. We have to think of the dependencies. The events without which, a whole lot of other things fall apart. So let's reverse that. What would fall apart, if a dependency were to be affected? Down in that temple dungeon thingy, when the Panditji was trying to kill me, I had time to think and listen to his history. He said his powers had started due to a ceremony performed in Varanasi. Could that be the dependency we need to push on?"

"That's right! He does say that," Josh said, flipping through his notebook. The sound of paper being ruffled came through the phone. "He said in his diary that he had gone to a Sadhu Ram Dharan, who had performed a ritual on the banks of the Ganges in Varanasi. So?"

"Well, I don't know where it will lead, but it seems to me that if some ceremony in Varanasi had made him so powerful, we should go there, to find out more. Do you think you could get away, Josh?"

"So you agree with me? That you can't run away from the Panditji?"

"I agree with you, Josh. And—I hate to admit this—you're totally right. We have to find a way to stop this guy, for the sake of my life, like you said, and also for the sake of my poor Daadi Ma and my father and his family. Oh my God, Josh, what are they going to say when they find out?"

"Actually, they know. I had to call your mom earlier, to try to find you."

"You did? They must be worried sick!"

She thanked him and ended the call quickly so she could talk to her parents and Daadi Ma. She dialed her home number urgently, unconcerned what time it must be in New Jersey.

"Are you okay?!" came her mother's voice immediately.

"Your friend is it, Josh, he called. We sit here all night!" Daadi Ma yelled in the background.

"Yes, Mom, yes, Daadi Ma, I'm okay. I promise."

"What has happened anyway, to the people of Maalpur? Uncouth!" her father chipped in.

"Hi, Dad. All right, if you have a minute, I can tell you what happened. It's kind of a long story."

The next day, Josh and Jaya found themselves in humid, crowded Varanasi airport. Stepping out of the plane, Jaya put on her black-rimmed sunglasses and turning to Josh, grabbed his hand and squeezed. Taking a big breath of air infused with engine exhaust, they crossed the tarmac on foot, entering the terminal through the sliding door, together.

The ride into the ancient city was a journey of increasingly narrow pathways, cobblestoned and interlocked. They were the same streets, in the same configurations, that had existed since the city's beginnings five thousand years ago. There was a point at which the taxi could no longer continue, so Josh and Jaya set off on foot, delicately sidestepping large olive-colored piles of cow dung. Jaya was carrying a hand-me-down teenager's backpack with two sets of clothes from Banita's charity pile and some basics she'd picked up at the airport. After her backpack had been stolen, she'd been wholly reliant on her grandmother's friends for creature comforts. Josh had his trusty mountaineering-styled pack, half filled with books he thought would be useful on their journey, the other half with flashlights and knives he'd picked up in the shops of Delhi. For protection, he'd said, and shrugged.

Now, standing in front of the Jasmine Hostel, Josh rang the buzzer once, twice, then a third time for good measure. Dusk was settling in, and the area was quiet as denizens rested for the day. Empty plastic chairs sat askew, recently vacated. A child of about ten was kicking a soccer ball repeatedly into a stone wall, returning his own rebound. Game over, he picked up the ball and ran back to his mother, who was standing in a doorway, calling him in for dinner. Just when Josh thought that they might need to find another place to stay, the wood-and-brass door opened with a loud crack. A youngish-looking man in a sweat-stained button-down shirt let them in.

"This way, this way," he said with a most perfunctory air as he tossed his jet-black hair.

Ushered inside, they quickly passed through the exchange of information at the desk: passports, names, credit cards. Upsells were lightly offered and graciously accepted for in-room Wi-Fi and morning roof-top yoga. A metal key three inches long and weighing nearly a quarter-pound was produced and bequeathed to them.

The second-floor room was nothing much to speak of. The windows were thick glass blocks, through which Jaya could just make out the Ganges below, if she angled her head just right— the river in the distance swirling like a snake in the darkening sky. An overhead streetlight illuminated the stone steps of the ghat leading down to the water.

Jaya sighed at the daunting task ahead of them. Searching for the Panditji's activities that may have occurred in Varanasi hundreds of years ago was the equivalent of using a digital Ouija board. She felt like she was attempting to communicate with a spirit whom she knew to be evil, which felt dangerous and wrong. Swallowing her discomfort, though, she encouraged Josh to continue. After all she was the one who had brought them here. It was too late to back out now.

Their first foray into the unknown started, of course, online, on Josh's computer. The Wi-Fi jerked them around, working in dribs and drabs. Their search for the term "ghat" returned results quite quickly, but the link entitled "Varanasi's Ghats: The Insider's Guide" loaded haphazardly, with whitespace slowly changing from empty boxes to images, in no particular order. The pictures came, filling the screen vertically from the top, in layers. Then the advertisements popped up, starting with an Indian airline's enticement to "Getaway to Kolkata: Rs 3099 this Sunday" in bright red letters. Ignoring the distractions as best they could, they huddled together on the disarmingly comfortable bed. The words, when they came, provided information but no insight.

"The ghats of Varanasi are essentially piers by which one can access the river waters. They are, in turns, a beautiful, disgusting, and life-changing experience," Jaya read aloud. *Oh, perfect*, she thought before continuing.

"Promising as much a religious awakening as they are open-air public baths, the ghats can be risky places, and this insider's guide recommends that the traveler take special precautions, beyond the usual advice to avoid pickpockets and to keep your valuables safe. As a tourist, you will be asked whether you would like to partake in the bathing ritual. Unfortunately, a small cottage industry of touts has sprung up, and tourists will be offered bathing towels, flip-flops, soap, even a bathing costume, for a small fee. Whether you take them up on their offer is, ultimately, a personal decision, but please do consider that the Ganges is said to be one of the most polluted bodies of water in the world, with many millions of tons of toxic sludge pouring in upstream from industrial towns further north and floating down to the river, untreated. The Ganges—along which millions of people conduct their daily lives using the water for bathing, drinking, and more—is not, despite what the touts will tell you, clean. Yes, progress has been made in recent years to clean up the river, but still, we urge our readers to strongly consider a boat ride instead of an actual bath to safely experience this most holy river.

"As for the ghats themselves, the Insider advises travelers to time their visits for the morning. Sunrise on the ghats is a once-in-a-lifetime experience, where you will see yogis performing their sun salutations and the faithful praying to their hearts' content. After dark, the ghats are to be strictly avoided with the exception of nightly rituals during major religious festivals, and then only accompanied by a local guide.

"Readers often ask whether they can make the journey alone, perhaps to find their own piece of solitude in this religious mecca. While it may be tempting, the Insider would not recommend it, and would advise hiring a guide from the hotel or a reputable tourist operator to take you to the right places and avoid touts. The Insider has received disturbing reports in recent months of tourists being surrounded and mugged by groups. For all of these reasons, visitors are strongly recommended to hire a guide to visit the river Ganges and the ghats."

"Well, okay then," Josh piped up. "Guess we need a guide."

"But what about the ghats themselves?" Jaya wondered, yawning, feeling exhausted. Her body was still recovering from her recent ordeal. A spot on her shoulder kept knotting up stubbornly, despite a massage from Josh at the Delhi airport. "How will we find the one where the Panditji did his ritual?"

"I wonder..." Josh murmured, typing "top 10 ghats" into the search engine. He muttered out loud as he scrolled through the results. "Sun Ghat, Moon Ghat, Washerman's Ghat, Women's Ghat… I don't know, Jaya, there doesn't seem to be much of anything."

He threw his best hypnotic gaze in the direction of his laptop, as if willing it to submit to his superior researcher's intuition to provide the guidance he needed, a trick that sometimes actually worked in his Delhi office. It was not to be.

"Any sound interesting to you, Jaya?" He turned when she didn't respond.

She had fallen asleep at his side, her arm lightly draped over his elbow, her head tucked two inches from his shoulder. He smiled, lifted a thick lock of her hair with a finger and let it fall. It occurred to him then that he was getting rather used to the lack of normalcy around her. His research project was off schedule, and here he was, away from the publisher's office, digging into a new project in the field. If he were being honest with himself, he might even admit he was sort of thrilled.

"So," Josh said, plopping into a chair next to Jaya, who was sipping a coffee and staring at a cement wall in the hotel's central open-air courtyard, "we have a guide coming at ten. I found the name of a ghat last night, and I think it might be a good place to start. Are you game?"

Jaya roused herself and finally noticed Josh's dark green eyes looking into hers. "Oh, oh, okay. What, um, what did you find?"

"I'll show you," he said. He grabbed his laptop from his backpack, pushed aside her coffee cup, and placed his device in the center of the table, flipping it open. He had to adjust the screen slightly to get the resolution just right in the already bright sunshine.

"See this?" he said, pointing to a list of ghats and their descriptions. He clicked on one of the items. "This is called the Kala Ghat. Look at its description." Jaya leaned in and read.

The Kala Ghat

The Kala Ghat is so named for the color black, referencing the black magic that is rumored to have been practiced here. It is now in disrepair and some miles from the main ghat activity in the center of town. It is said to be haunted, and locals refuse to visit it after dark. Whether one believes these stories or not, it is true that at one time, the ghats along the Ganges were more active than they are today, with many more ghats stretching miles in either direction from the center of the main ghat activity. Despite its eerie name, this ghat will disappoint visitors for their troubles. The actual Kala Ghat as of this writing is hardly viable as a bathing venue, as the steps no longer connect to the river banks. If you go, bring your own food and water, and prepare for at least a few hours journey there and back.

"So we go here and then what?" Jaya asked.

"Well, you said the Panditji worked with a sadhu, right? The one who was teaching him all that stuff he learned in Varanasi. Don't you think he must have learned these things, well, somewhere like this? I mean, this is an ancient city, but some things don't change that quickly," Josh said.

"It's true—things change slowly in India. It's such an old place. And people hang on to their traditions. So, you're saying that we..." Jaya started.

"I'm saying if we find the location of where he might have been, we're a bit closer," Josh said, finishing her sentence.

"This Kala Ghat, how do we know it's the one?" Jaya asked.

"Because I looked through all the other ghat descriptions on this list. There are like, thirty of them. This is the only one that remotely sounded like a ghat where a sadhu would be teaching things that counter the rules of life of itself."

"I guess it sort of fits," Jaya said. "If the Panditji was learning from this disreputable sadhu, and he was learning to mess with the basics of life and death, that would be rather blasphemous. Or black magic, as they say. Then yeah, I guess it's possible."

"So, let's start there," Josh said, smiling, satisfied with his morning's research. He reached out and squeezed her shoulder before he could stop himself.

Soon after, Josh and Jaya met their guide, Bajrang, at the front desk. A native of Varanasi and recently retired, the former adjunct university professor had so far enjoyed his newfound career as a tour guide. He even dressed the part, with a smart brown safari-style jacket, loose cotton pants, and a pair of hiking boots purchased on a recent trip to Thailand. Still intensely energetic at nearly sixty-five, Bajrang radiated positive joy at showing visitors the sights and sounds of the city he had known since childhood. He only wished sometimes that the tourists were more adventurous. Most tread the same well-worn routes, asked similar questions, and stopped at the same spots for pictures. It was with great surprise, therefore, that he welcomed Jaya and Josh's strange request to take them past the main sights and a few miles outside the hubbub to look at a disused ghat with a bad reputation. He looked at the couple anew, as if to assess their fitness for such a detour. They evidenced no particular markers of being obsessed with the occult. They clearly did not seem confused about what they were asking, as Josh had pulled him aside to show him the info on his computer and specifically asked for the Kala Ghat. Bajrang could not fathom what attachment, what whim, might have originated this wish. But, considering that his tours the rest of the week would be to the same three ghats, edging past the same set of ten lurking touts, he took this request and its uniqueness with the enthusiasm and professionalism it deserved.

"It is long to walk," he said to them. "But for me"—here he put his hands on his chest to emphasize his energy— "it is no problem. Good for health!"

He firmly insisted that they purchase overpriced bottled waters from the front desk, after which the party crossed the threshold into the main street. Josh had a slight white sheen to his face and arms where he'd lathered on sunscreen. Jaya peered into the sky and put on her sunglasses and a hat for good measure. Then they both quickly shuffled after Bajrang.

"Here is the touristic ghats!" their guide said as soon as they approached the crowded ghats that he would return to later this week. "See all the people for the bathing. This is most sacred duty of a Hindu. And. Look there. There is the buffalo herd taking cool bath. The mother, she is a river, she is a comfort to all the peoples and even to the animals."

As they walked past, a group of five grayish black water buffalo with curved horns lounged just barely submerged in the water. A rail-thin minder frolicked nearby. As they watched, the minder lightly swatted a buffalo with a twig switch. The buffalo responded by letting its long tail loose, swooping over the top side of its back. Tail parried with switch. The group kept walking.

The Kala Ghat, upon first inspection a few hours later, was as broken down as advertised. Peering down the hill where they were standing, there wasn't much to see besides the water below. About twenty crumbling stone steps and an equally decrepit square platform formed the ghat. Ever the academic, Bajrang insisted that they walk down with him to see it up-close. Shrugging, Josh headed down the uneven surface, holding Jaya's hand to ensure she didn't slip in her sandals. The air became thicker as they descended. Josh visibly shivered. Jaya rubbed her neck where goosebumps had formed. Bajrang looked at both of them and raised an eyebrow, mimicking with his body the heavy feeling that permeated the area. Something bad had happened here; lingering now was a sinister and dense air. Jaya felt the physical sensation that her chest was being pushed down by a vise, making it difficult to breathe. When they had assembled on a stone platform at the base of the ghat, Josh threw his arm around Jaya's back to steady them both.

"Now," Bajrang said, with an academic air, "this is Kala Ghat. 'Kala,' you see, means the color of black. Now, in this place the peoples, you know, the sadhus, were having these rituals that were not allowed by the king's temples. They were performing rituals against the teachings of our most holy scriptures. The sadhus, they were, how do you say? They were outcasts from the society. So? They did not worship our gods. They worshipped... Jayaji, can you guess? No? That is, they worshipped? Yama. Now. Who is Yama? Joshji, you I think will not be knowing this. Yama is? God of Death. He is in form of? Buffalo. He takes the peoples who have died to be cremated."

"So he's a death dealer?" Josh asked.

"That is correct," Bajrang said, beaming at his wise student.

"These people here, they are, the evil sadhus. They were making? The Black. Magic. Ceremony." Here Bajrang punctuated every word dramatically. Years of keeping bored students awake in lecture halls had given him a natural theatrical flair. "Here was the worship of? Yama. Unclean. Impure. Dirty. Not? For the good peoples."

Jaya's nerves were jumpy. This place was wild, unkempt. They were miles away from the core of Varanasi, and there were eerily few people anywhere in the vicinity. This was a place she did not want to get lost in, especially if rituals were being performed.

"But," Jaya started, "it doesn't seem like that's still going on? It's not, right? I mean this place looks empty to me."

As she said that, a loud rumble of several car engines grew closer and closer. They all turned their heads upwards and saw a convoy of four jeeps roll up to the Kala Ghat. From what Jaya could tell, at least ten people energetically jumped out and started unloading gear where their small tour group had been standing earlier. She blinked.

"It looks like a film crew," Josh said, peering at the black crates.

"Film industry. It is called? Bollywood. It is? Largest film industry in world," Bajrang said, not missing a beat. Bajrang, for one, was already thrilled by the unique request to come to this ghat, and was now further intrigued by this new commotion. He stretched and sighed and planted his feet firmly on the ground, hoping that Josh and Jaya wouldn't rush him along.

As they stood watching, a tall man with floppy blackish-brown hair and noticeably pale skin approached them. He was followed by a twentysomething blond male assistant holding an umbrella over the tall man's head, and another twentysomething tiny, dark-haired female assistant holding a water bottle in one hand and a clipboard in another that she kept looking down to refer to.

"G'day," the tall man said in a thick Australian accent, "admiring your bravery at coming all the way down to the Kala Ghat. Actually, our film crew told us not to come down here. Said the whole place was evil."

The female assistant handed him the water bottle and a blue hankie; he took a swig and wiped his face. The male assistant adjusted the umbrella slightly, to shield his charge from the noonday sun. The film star, as the group realized he must be, was in his early thirties and wore a pair of creased, faded-blue jeans, a rough-looking pair of dark brown hiking boots, and a loose tank top in olive green. Voluminous amounts of chest hair peeked up from the tank top. The effect could be described, as Josh would call it later, as hiker-punk.

"Funny. You can see we're still alive. I'm Josh, by the way. This is Jaya. And Bajrang, our guide."

"Ah, you're American," the film star said, pegging Josh's accent. "So that's why you haven't asked for a selfie. Today's your lucky day. Well then," he strode forward, faster than the umbrella assistant could keep up, "this is where we're filming, eh? We're on a quest. To find the most haunted places in India. Don't worry, mate, I won't hit on your girl." He proceeded to wink at Jaya and grip Josh's hand in a firm handshake. He gave a deep namaste to Bajrang, who returned it with a crooked grin. The man was a whirlwind of confidence. "Back home they know me as Dan Katt. Look me up, mate. Dan Katt. Film star."

CHAPTER ELEVEN

Jaya's Story

Accustomed to being the center of attention, Bajrang jumped in to introduce himself to Dan Katt. "I am guide, Bajrang, local for this area, from Varanasi. Teacher in the university, retired. Now, I teach tourists and visitors like you, about our culture. This place, Varanasi, it is something different from any other place in the world!"

"Would you be willing to be interviewed? For our viewers? We want to know, you know, the history of this place, the Kala Ghat," Dan asked, getting straight to the point. He knew a character when he saw one.

As he spoke, Jaya's memory was jogged. She turned and whispered to Josh, "His name, remember, Josh? The bartender in Goa was telling us about a Dan Katt. The hunter of weird mysteries or something."

Josh's eyes widened in recognition.

Bajrang, meanwhile, was trying to contain himself. He nodded immediately, giving his consent to being filmed while frowning to try to control his enthusiastic smile.

"Could you sign the release form?" The clipboard assistant stepped forward, ready to get Bajrang's signature.

"This is? A form for you to use my video?" Bajrang asked, as he accepted the pen. He signed straight away, before the question was even answered, still gazing in admiration at Dan Katt. Amid a whirl of papers and microphones and wires, Bajrang was soon hooked up to a headset, and a camera was turned on and directed at him.

"We're here at the Kala Ghat, with a local guide from the heart of Varanasi. Bajrang has been a teacher, a professor, and an observer of human society in Varanasi his whole life. He's an absolute expert about this place, and as luck would have it, I happened to find him here, today, at the Kala Ghat. I swear to you, this is not scripted. We'll leave the faux meet-ups to the reality dating shows. On my show you only get the uncut truth. This is really happening, right now," Dan narrated into the camera. "Bajrang, tell us if you would, about the history of this place we're standing in now. And, for our viewers back home, is it still in use?"

Bajrang started in a roundabout way, taking a deep breath and puffing up his safari-suited chest as he began. "Nehruji? He is? First prime minister of India. This is when? Varanasi government closed this place. The government came and put a lock, a tala, on the door to the temple here. And? They took away the sadhus, far away. Because they were finding bad things here. Dead bodies. Drugs. Superstitious people. From this times, this Kala Ghat is? Empty. Finish. Khatam, as you say in Hindi." He punctuated each word by crossing his arms in an X, the universal symbol of something coming to an end.

After an afternoon's worth of shooting, Dan Katt was relaxing in a tent his crew had installed. With a cigarette dangling from his mouth, he was rocking back and forth in his camp chair so that his knees tipped up slightly. Jaya, Josh, and Bajrang were seated in a semi-circle around Dan, breathing in the stale air of the midafternoon.

"So," he said, "you've seen now, the sort of show I do. We travel the world seeking the weird and the cool, then we film it." As he finished speaking, one hand shot out into the air, expectantly awaiting an assistant to place a cold beer in it. His request was quickly granted. Cold drinks were also tossed to his new companions, who accepted them gratefully.

"Lucky, I found you all, mates," Dan said, "especially you, Bajrang. Mate, without you I don't know that my show would have been that good."

"But, may I ask?" Bajrang said, sitting forward. "All this time I am a guide, and no one has been asking for this Kala Ghat. Sir, how did you find this place?"

Jaya had to admit, she was curious about this as well. It seemed like a wild moment of serendipity that Dan Katt was here, at the exact same moment that she and Josh had chosen to visit. While she was still feeling sheepish about dragging Josh to Varanasi, and then for dragging him to this ghat, all in the search for some ephemeral trace of the Panditji, Dan's presence was validating her decision.

"A lark really," Dan said breezily. "Our crew was driving from our last stop in Goa cross-country to a temple on the border of Nepal, where the locals claim that every night a statue of Buddha awakens. Anyway, we were here for the night, in Varanasi. And you think, well hell, this city? It just feels old. Right? Varanasi is an old place. Has to be something here for us to film. Of course, there were the ghats and the cremations and so forth on the river and the dead bodies. That's standard. What I'm looking for is stuff my viewers won't have seen. So, we posed the question to our viewers. We ran a little contest, asked them to find the creepiest thing that they wanted us to check out here in Varanasi. Sort of threw it out to the mob, as it were. And this is what came back. Here we are."

"Oh, Goa!" Jaya said. "We were just there, Josh and I. In fact, we met Ricki the bartender there, and he told us about you, Dan. I guess I didn't expect to meet you here, in real life, in the middle of nowhere."

"Ricki! That man is bloody sick mate. You stopped at The Pub, did you? That's good peoples. But why did he mention me? Don't tell me you've got something weird?"

"Weird isn't the word for it," Josh started.

He and Jaya made eye contact. Would they or wouldn't they? Josh was willing to let Jaya determine the next move. After all, the Panditji's secret was hers to tell. Jaya nodded slightly to Josh and grabbed his hand, for good measure. She was feeling even-keeled, which was no small thing after what she had been through, and hopeful for the first time since this whole adventure began. Perhaps having someone like Dan Katt, an international film star, on her side could be helpful. Even just the fact that he had fans worldwide, people following him, could be a counter to the thousands of yoga disciples that the Panditji had amassed over the years, all over the world. Meeting Josh, who had already done so much for her, and now Dan meant that Jaya wouldn't be all alone, fighting this fight. The Panditji wouldn't be able to hide his deeds, nor would he be able to disappear or harm her, without others knowing. There was strength in that, and Jaya took solace in it.

"Josh is right, weird isn't the word. The word you want is... evil," Jaya said with finality.

"Now, *this* is something I have to hear." Dan whooped in excitement.

"Friends," Bajrang said, looking uncomfortable, "I think this is not the moment, for such a tale. It is bad luck, to be talking of such evil, in such a bad place with its bad history. You will all please come, to my house. Just wait one minute." He whipped out an industrial-looking phone from his front pocket and punched one button rather decisively. A conversation, evidently with his wife, transpired. Tilting his head to one side in the Indian way, Bajrang said, "You will just come. Maybe we go in half-hour. Sir," he turned to Dan, "we can use your driver?"

Dan responded with a thumbs-up. It was on.

They arrived at Bajrang's home after passing through a series of wide, well-paved roads lined with houses, each with low walls surrounding the property. Upon entry, they were seated on a covered veranda that adjoined the front door and served orange sherbet by Bajrang's wife, Simi. Wearing a turquoise salwar kameez, Simi was slight, with her hair in a long braid and an intelligent grin on her face. Like her husband, she seemed entirely mesmerized and enthused by life. Her new visitors would certainly keep her entertained.

Jaya had slipped off her sandals and was enjoying the hard, cool marble floor tickling her feet. As she began telling her story, her drink lay untouched, dripping condensation onto the glass table.

Jaya started at the beginning. She explained how her Daadi Ma had sent her to India to see her family's land, and what the PKM Ashram was like. When she mentioned the Panditji's name, Bajrang nodded. He was familiar with it, yes, he said. Completely in sync with her, Josh pulled out the book when she got to that part of the story. After what had happened to Jaya, he had carried it with him everywhere. Josh stepped in now, seamlessly, to describe what he'd translated, and how the book was a sort of diary of the Panditji's life. Picking back up from Josh, Jaya explained what they had learned: that the Panditji had used a ceremony at a ghat in Varanasi, perhaps even the one they had just been to, hundreds of years ago, conducted by a sadhu who claimed to be able to return the power of life and death back to a disciple.

Bajrang gasped. "Hai Ram, but how could this be? He would have to break the cycle of reincarnation!" He said it first in Hindi, and then again in English for his guests, and he patted his forehead with his handkerchief. Simi looked on with concern, at him and their visitors. She produced a string of prayer beads from a pocket of her shirt, which Bajrang wordlessly picked up, and began to nervously count.

It was at this point that Dan urgently called for his assistant, who was waiting in the car. He needed to have this all in notes. He knew then, without question, that he and his crew would be staying in Varanasi for a while. The mystery of the awakening Buddha statue could wait. There was a real mystery here for him to investigate.

Sensing Jaya's hesitation, Josh filled in the fact that the Panditji's diary wasn't just about one life, but in fact lives, plural. Every time, he reverted to the ashram and wrote another entry. When Josh got to the part about Jaya's kidnapping by the Panditji and the attempted murder, Simi gasped. Jaya clutched Josh's hand weakly as he spoke, but she was glad that he was telling them about this. She didn't want Dan or Bajrang or anyone else to help her, without knowing that they themselves could be at risk. And that's what she told them now. She'd understand if they didn't want anything to do with her. After all, she was drawing great evil to them already, to her gracious hosts, and to Dan, without having any control of it. For that, she felt sorry.

"Jayaji," Simi said in Hindi, "you can tell your friends what I'm saying. This Kala Ghat and the Panditji. My family has been in Varanasi for a long time. We are Brahmins. Brahmin people know things that the lay people do not. This Kala Ghat, it was closed as Bajrang told you in the time after Independence. It was mostly a place of ill repute, where sadhus and cheats and touts took advantage of desperate people who would do anything to bring back their loved ones from the dead, people who would flout the rules of dharma, of life itself, to avoid any temporary pain.

"And this Panditji, his sadhu he found to help him, well, it could have been any one of the holy men operating around there. We used to hear stories about people like him when I was a girl, but we thought they were not real, they were just stories to scare us. One of the nannies who used to watch the children during the day used to say that if we were bad, we would be sent to this sadhu, and he would harm us and take away our childhoods and make us cry."

After Jaya relayed what Simi had said to the group in English, Dan jumped up in excitement.

"But that settles it! We'll have a show, won't we? To explore the history of this reincarnation ceremony, here, at the Kala Ghat. Surely the two things are close enough—the ceremony *could* have happened there, that's enough for our viewers. And maybe, we can even take a trip to Maalpur after that and meet this Panditji of yours, Jaya. We can take him by surprise! Get him on camera. Broadcast his misdeeds to the world! He won't go free, I promise you."

Bajrang beamed. This day was turning out to be the most entertaining since his retirement. "I would be happy, Mr. Dan, to guide you, in your quest."

"Jaya's quest, you mean. After all, Jaya, you're the star of this show. Are you comfortable with all of this? You know, being on film, telling your story?" Dan asked her.

Jaya took a beat, thought for a moment, and said, "Why not? I was almost poisoned and had to run away and more. And

I think people need to know. Especially all of those followers of the Panditji's. I worry for my friends, like Barb and Angie, who are still there. You know? He could really hurt someone, even kill them. He's done it before, and he will do it again. And I could never let that sit on my conscience. Bajrang, Simi, Dan? You want to help? Let's do this."

"Sir!" The driver, in his crisp white uniform and cloth-covered cap, stood stiffly in front of Ravi and the Panditji and saluted. The two lovers were lounging in bed, eating a carton of late-season mangos, recently sent in from Mumbai.

"And?" Ravi asked expectantly, wiping the pulp on his hands with a towel.

"Confirmed, sir. One Jaya Gupta left via the Maalpur train station to Delhi. 20:30 last night."

"Thank you, driver," Ravi sighed, handing him a stack of rupees. "This should cover it, no?" He was referring to the bribe paid for the information that the driver had procured.

"Yes, of course. Um, sir?" the driver said. He was still standing in the entryway of the room, refusing to leave.

"What is it?" the Panditji asked haughtily, with the lip of a mango skin hanging from his mouth.

"Sir, also I was able to find out the onward journey sir, from the train station. It seems at 10:50 this morning, Ms. Jaya Gupta has boarded a local flight leaving Delhi airport—"

"What does this mean!" the Panditji snapped impatiently. "That she has gone? Ravi, you promised that she would not leave."

Ravi gulped. If Jaya had indeed absconded from the country, they would have big problems. He and the Panditji were quite enjoying this life. Their international fame had never been greater. The ashram never more luxurious. Jaya exposing them might necessitate an early exit from this life, and Ravi was loath to do that too soon. Especially, he thought, when his current body was in such good shape. He stretched a leg idly, admiring the muscle tone that he'd achieved.

"Driver," Ravi said, still staring at his legs. "Did you happen to find out where she went, from Delhi?"

"Sir, yes, but—"

"But what?"

"Sir, the information will require another 2,000 rupees."

"Oh, here you go!" Ravi said, throwing his wallet at the driver. The driver took the money and stepped outside, finally, to make a phone call. The Panditji pulled Ravi close to him, leaning in for a kiss.

"You'll find her, right, Ravi my dear? We can't let her get away, this one. She's trouble."

"Of course. Once we find her, we'll stick her underneath the deepest rock underneath the Shiva temple. That problematic, nosy woman will be out of the way. These foreigners bring nothing but complications."

"Mmm good," the Panditji said.

"Sirs!" the driver said, returning from his call. "I have found the informations. A Ms. J. Gupta left Delhi airport this morning and arrived, at 1200 hours, to—"

"Spit it out!" the Panditji said, impatient.

"Varanasi airport, sir. She arrived in Varanasi. And sirs? They said she was not alone. Someone was with her."

CHAPTER TWELVE

Living History

n the week following Jaya's escape, there was chaos at the ashram, which was not in keeping with its usual calm, sophisticated air. Barb and Angie were surprised at first, and then deeply upset. How could Jaya have disappeared like that? Angie had insisted that Ravi take them to the police station to file a report, though she didn't have much hope that it would be successful. The rest of the students in the cohort spent a tense day unable to concentrate on yoga, waiting for Jaya to return, or for some sign that she was alive.

It was just as well, because the Panditji, furious that she had escaped, had lost his temper, making himself ill and canceling all classes. He had holed up in his room, eating mangoes with Ravi, until they learned that Jaya was in Varanasi. Ravi, ever the faithful helpmate and lover, announced to the students that, for the first time in the PKM Ashram's history, they would be canceling the rest of the ashram's yoga session. Of course, he explained, there would be a money back guarantee, but the students must pack up and leave as soon as possible. Lilly would arrange any international transfers to ensure they had as little hassle as possible.

"It's Jaya!" Angie said, staring at her phone. She and Barb and a few other students were at the airport in Mumbai, ensconced in one of the lounges and awaiting their flights back home.

"Are you okay, Jaya? Oh my God, please, please tell us you're okay? We're all sitting at the airport." Barb spoke quickly into Angie's speakerphone.

Jaya gulped. Listening to Barb and Angie made it real for her. How many thousands of students just like them had come into contact with this dangerous man over the years, putting their faith in him as their yogic teacher and spiritual leader without knowing his big secret. Oh sure, perhaps some like Angie knew about his secret lover, Ravi, or could guess; the even bigger secret was one that was utterly beyond imagination. How many students had unknowingly introduced the Panditji to someone in their network that he could have poisoned to meet his own ends? How many people had the Panditji and Ravi actually conspired to murder over the years?

"I'm in Varanasi, with that guy, Josh. I promise, it's all okay— Wait, why are you at the airport?" Jaya asked. Josh was sitting next to her, a pillar of moral support. Barb and Angie filled her in, about how the Panditji had gone on a search for her and then had abruptly canceled the semester and sent them home. At that, Jaya inhaled sharply, making a squeaking sound that came out like a yelp.

"We can come to you, Jaya, seriously. We could detour to Varanasi and make sure you're okay!" Barb said, concerned about the panic she sensed on the other end. "Anyway we've got time to burn since neither Angie nor I were planning to go home so soon."

"It's okay, guys," she said, smiling at Josh. "It's better you go back home. Look, I can't tell you everything right now, but I'm in the middle of something and I need to finish this. No, I promise, it's okay, really. It's just, the Panditji, he's dangerous. Like, really, not a good person. Go home. It's better this way. When I come up for air, I'll tell you everything. But in the meantime, I'm serious, stay away from the Panditji and any of his people. He's bad news."

"Wait," Angie said, "you said you were in Varanasi, right? Because that's where the Panditji said he was going. I overheard him and Ravi talking about it, right before they shut down the ashram. Jaya, are you sure that your disappearance and them closing the ashram isn't connected somehow? It's a pretty big coincidence, don't you think? And the Panditji, all these years and I don't remember him ever shutting the ashram down before. He lives for his students."

Jaya only heard that the Panditji was coming to Varanasi. That meant that he must know, somehow, that she was here. Fear shot through her. She felt trapped again. Her head pulsed. Even here, she thought, even here, with Josh and her new friends, Dan Katt and Bajrang, she wasn't safe.

Just as the Panditji and Ravi were arriving in Varanasi's train station, on the other side of town Jaya and Josh were in the main bazaar eating lunch with Dan Katt. Before them were deep-fried kachori stuffed with potato and other vegetables, and stainless-steel cups of steaming sweet tea, which were too hot to touch and which Dan insisted on spiking with alcohol he had stashed in a bottle in one of his jacket pockets.

There was a world out there, on the street, that they watched silently. A hunched man, bow-legged, occasionally leaned his head out his doorway two inches to spit the red liquid of betel leaf and tobacco. To his right, the vendor he'd purchased the concoction from was doing a brisk after-lunch business from a wooden cabinet mounted on a rolling cart. He methodically picked a betel leaf, slathered it with a mauve paste, filled it with various fixings from small, clear plastic boxes, wrapped the leaf in aluminum foil, and handed it to the customer. People went by. Men with thick rings on their fingers. Women holding their saris delicately over their eyes, to shield their faces from the midday sun. Children in school uniforms proudly flipping their oiled and braided hair. Farmers running buffaloes to and from their daily haunts.

The restaurant where they sat was in a casual cafeteria style. It had floors of tamped-down mud and a sign in Hindi script that incongruously said, "Varanasi Guest House," despite its having no rooms to let. A fine mist of oil dissipated into the heated air as big cooking vats bubbled. Everything in here seemed older than time itself. Which it probably was, given that Varanasi, or Kashi as it had been named in ancient times, had been a functioning city for thousands of years. In fact, anything did seem possible, including but not limited to her experience at the Kala Ghat.

"So," Jaya said.

"So?" Josh asked.

"So what do we do now?"

"Fuck if I know, love," Dan added.

"Can I just say," Jaya said, getting a new caffeine-and-sugar kick from the spiked sweet tea, "that this is all a bit surreal? You guys, me, this," she waved her arm around expansively, "the Panditji. Never in a million years would I have guessed all this would happen, when Daadi Ma wheedled me into coming to India."

"I'm enjoying it to be honest," Josh countered thoughtfully. "I thought, you know, I'd come out here, do my stint in Delhi, do this research, write this book. All I was focused on, when I met you on the plane, was getting this research out the door. And now? Look at me. I've asked my publisher for a six-month extension."

"Josh! You didn't!" Jaya exclaimed.

"Didn't what?" he said, innocently.

"You delayed your work for me?" she asked, smiling despite herself.

"Come on, Jaya. How are we supposed to get to the bottom of all of this with me in Delhi? It can't be done. This is too interesting. No, scratch that. *You* are too interesting." Josh couldn't believe those words had just come out of his mouth.

"No, but that's good," Dan said. "You guys, this is MASSIVE. A place that does perverted magic in the heart of India? And now, proof that this Panditji cat has gained control over reincarnation here? We can stretch this episode out. Make a second one, heck even a third. Josh mate, how could you possibly stay doing whatever it was you were doing? Wait, what was it you were doing again?" He snapped his fingers a few times.

"Researching the connections between Russian and Sanskrit languages—but that can wait. At least a little while. After all, they've waited this long. If I'm lucky, I won't get scooped."

"This is all great, you all. Fascinating for you," Jaya said. "For me, I'm terrified. This man, no, he's not a man. He's something else. A being? A superhuman? Subhuman? Whatever. This thing has been living around my family for years, for generations. You know that weird feeling at the Kala Ghat, that heavy air? I feel that heavy cloud following us."

Dan Katt took a drag from a recently lit joint, apparently it had been stashed in another side pocket all along. No one in the restaurant paid the group any attention. Shock value, ultimately, does attenuate down to zero, if one sums up all the actions of mankind over a long enough period of time.

Jaya and Josh had moved from the Jasmine Hostel into Dan's place a few days back. It was spectacular. The grounds were a dense forest: bamboo, palm, fig trees. And so many types of flowers and leaves. Crisp leaves with light pink outlines. Forked leaves shaped like snowflakes. Hardy, brushy-looking leaves. Leaves that framed magenta flowers. Flowers whose petals were geometrically shaped. The house itself shone white with the ministrations of its head butler and his staff, its rectangular lines reflecting in the mid-morning sun. Three marble steps led to a raised foyer. The main room was bisected by a fountain surrounded by a small garden. From there, a range of rooms lay spread out over two floors. The back of the house spilled out through two French doors to a cool blue inground swimming pool and a large awning.

A question of what to do next had been eating at Jaya for days, and now, sitting with Josh in front of the pool, she had an idea.

"Josh, can you get your notebook? I want to hear that one passage again."

"Sure thing," he said, hopping off his chair to rifle through his backpack in the corner of the room.

Returning, he settled back in and passed the notebook to Jaya. She found the page and read:

"'There was a ritual performed by Sadhu Ram Dharan at the ghats of Varanasi. It gave me control over my own death and eventual return, that is my own reincarnation. I arranged also to have my faithful assistant and lover, Ravi Kumar, perform this ceremony, so we could be together for all time. This recording shall serve witness and continuity, should that I forget.'

"Okay, so we found the ghat, right?" Jaya continued.

"Yeah, pretty sure," Josh said. "Pretty sure, based on what Bajrang's wife said."

"What does your researcher's intuition tell you?"

"Well," he said, more cautiously than was typical for him. "I guess this would have all taken place in the 1600s, so there's likely to be some written record. India had a culture of written literature. Not to mention that there are people, you know, charged with keeping records. Priestly families, that sort of thing. I think it's possible that someone connected to the religious community here might somewhere, somehow know something about this."

"India is a big place, too," Jaya added. "The scale of this place. There are a lot of subcultures. Pockets of things happening that the police or government would ignore. I think it's possible, too. So we find the priestly families. I think that's obvious. We make a list. We interview them. We check them off."

"Okay, but where will we find these people?" Josh asked. "I mean, your plan sounds doable but how will we find them?"

"What about our tour guide?"

"Bajrang? You think?"

"Didn't he say he worked at a university, before he retired to become a tour guide?"

"You know what? Yeah. We start with him."

"Think this will work?" Jaya asked.

"Well, if it doesn't, do you think it would stop Dan from telling the most hyperbolic story possible?" Josh joked.

Later that week, Jaya, Josh, Bajrang, and Simi found themselves stuffed uncomfortably into the back of a 1970s-era Ambassador of light green hue, with Dan sitting shotgun and Jaya practically on Josh's lap next to Bajrang and Simi. They were off to meet a Brahmin acquaintance of Simi's, who she felt might know something. Helmed by Dan's driver, the Ambassador deftly weaved its way past the crowded city center and onto a highway, expertly avoiding two speeding teenagers on a scooter going the wrong way and a stoic farmer hogging the road with a giant wooden cart full of hay. In due time, they arrived at a dark brown metal door, cut into a cement wall, with a tiled marble sign bearing the names of its primary residents: M. Rao, V.S. Rao.

Incapable of silence, Dan insisted on talking, to no one in particular, the whole way from the car to the entrance and into the house, while the rest willfully ignored him. Simi, who had her braid covered today with a scarf that matched a gray salwar kameez, led the way, her hands clasped firmly in namaste, as they were shown into a formal sitting room. They heard the chugging sounds of an air conditioner and noticed how the lilac hues of the fluorescent lights caught the sunlight and threw color on the blue walls. The effect was altogether calming. Still, the party sat stiffly on the short couches and graciously accepted the cold orange drinks that were brought in for them, rising as soon as Simi's friend, Mr. Rao, walked in.

Mr. Rao was in his eighties. A heavyset man, he wore a white dhoti, and a purple cloth with white stripes was laid over his bare, fleshy shoulders. He also wore the cross-body thread signaling that he was a Brahmin.

"Hello, I am Mr. Rao," he said, directing this at Dan and Josh primarily, and nodding at Jaya. "Tell me, Simiji, what are your guests from foreign seeking to know?"

Simi took a deep breath, and Bajrang looked absently at the floor while sucking down his orange soda with a slurp. She began. Despite her conversing in classic Hindi with its Sanskrit loan words, nearly all the English speakers in the room caught the phrases "sadhu" and "Kala Ghat" and the words' subsequent effect on Mr. Rao. His mood changed in a flash, from solicitous to slightly irate. Bajrang winced as Mr. Rao started to speak loudly, questioning why it was that Simi and he had brought this line of discussion into his house. The only person unaffected by this display was Dan, who sat with a strange and inappropriately sublime grin, absolutely engrossed in the entertainment value of it all.

Jaya thought she might die of shame. *What have I gotten these nice people into? Why? And for what? After all, wouldn't the Panditji eventually fade away? Why not just leave it alone?* Too far in to turn back now, she was incredibly relieved when Bajrang stood up to go.

"Please, there is no need for this, sir," Bajrang announced, upset. "You? Have no need for tension. Everyone please relax. Come, Simi. Dan, Jaya, Josh! We must be going!"

Once outside the house, Bajrang broke it down for them. "Yes, well. It seems our friend Mr. Rao is? Not to tell any informations about the Kala Ghat. He is denying his knowledge *most* strongly. He is not knowing any Kala Ghat, any sadhu. This is? Dead end. No options," he said, shaking his head and swaying his whole body in denial. "My friends, I am sorry."

"So..." Jaya said, "that's it?" She was slightly bewildered that the gregarious Bajrang wasn't more interested in pushing this further. Out of the corner of her eye, she could see Dan arrogantly folding himself back into the car, dramatically angry that he hadn't gotten the lead to take the episode further.

"Bas. Enough," Bajrang said. "Nothing to be done. He says? He does not know. We cannot force him. There is nothing more, what can we do?" He looked sad as he added, "It has been good tour for you, I hope. India is? Big place. Many people. All live together. Your Panditji, he has the space to live. And you. Everyone in harmony. Better not to take tension. Ignore. Continue to live life. Mr. Dan Katt, sir," he spoke to Dan through an open window, "you must ask for my help, some other way. Jayaji, Joshji, thank you, it has been a pleasure to meet you."

And with a deep namaste, Bajrang and Simi walked off in the opposite direction. Whatever bank of curiosity and hospitality they had to give had been depleted.

Dan, Josh, Jaya, and Dan's girlfriend, Nisha, were sitting around a heavy wooden table at his house the evening after the failed trip with Bajrang and Simi, trying to figure out what to do next. His crew leads Lou and Erin had joined too; Erin, in a long flowing head scarf, was scribbling the ideas down on a large piece of paper, on an easel in the drawing room.

The ideas included:

man-on-the-street interviews,

a trip to Maalpur,

and lurking around the Kala Ghat to interview anyone who came by.

"This doesn't feel right," Jaya said. "I fear we're just grasping here."

"You," Nisha said, turning to Josh and pointing with her bright red fingernail, "were you planning to come to Varanasi you said, for your research? You said that, right?"

"Yeah, actually. Good memory. But not for a while though..." Josh said.

"So, you have a list? Of people to interview? Intellectual people?"

"I... guess, yeah. What are you thinking?"

"Oh, I get it," Jaya jumped in. "We interview those people. Like what we tried to do with Mr. Rao, only that didn't work, but maybe... maybe there are others. Other people who know something about the past."

"Exactly!" Nisha said, smiling. "Problem solved. Get this list. Surely, some of these people will come from families that have some knowledge of this sadhu or your Panditji. After all, this place is rather provincial. Not at all like my native Mumbai. People stay here for years, you know. Never leave, for generations." Nisha was the wealthy, pampered daughter of a major Bollywood movie producer. When she and Dan first got together, people talked. She resented the implication that she might be dating him to break into the Australian movie scene, which she felt was nowhere near the preeminent place for someone of her stature. Dan, for his part, took high offense to the idea that he needed the funding from her rich father to keep his worldwide reality documentary series running. The truth was, the only reason they were together was good old fashioned lust. Beguiling and bejeweled, with long dark brown hair down to her mid-waist, she was a sight to behold, especially in her cut-off short shorts. They were now well into their sixth month together, but Dan's crew still treated the whole romance with skepticism. This wasn't the first time their boy Dan had done this. There had been his fling in South Africa, then in Peru, and now in India.

"Right," Josh said, surprised that Nisha's idea didn't sound half-bad. "I'll call Amrita right away. She's like my local fixer in Delhi. Dan, your crew, you would like her. Anyway, I wasn't supposed to be in Varanasi until later in my research schedule, but I'm sure she can rustle up the interview list early."

Jaya felt a deep sense of relief. Even knowing that the Panditji might be here, in Varanasi, looking for her this very minute, she could at least take comfort in all of these people, her newfound friends, pulling for her. They were all trying to help her, to protect her. When she'd left New York, she couldn't have imagined meeting even one new friend, let alone a sort-of boyfriend and two new girlfriends and a film star. That seemed like years ago and miles away now.

That night the sky broke with heavy rain and thunder, and Varanasi flooded. The Panditji and Ravi, staying in a traditional guesthouse for religious folk near the ghats, watched the rain in silence, cuddled together on the bed. The Panditji was calm now, but he had not been earlier today.

You see, earlier that day, while Josh, Jaya, and Dan were hitting a dead end with Mr. Rao, the Panditji and Ravi had gone to visit the home of a prominent Brahmin family. This distinguished gentleman told them the most eye-popping story, about a ragtag group of foreigners including an Australian film star who were producing a show about the Kala Ghat. He was concerned, he recounted, that the modern world had allowed for such crossing of cultures. It would not do, he said, for too many of India's mysteries to be discovered, and that too, by a foreigner. He lamented that the times were changing. India, she too was changing. Foreign people could go anywhere, find anything. They could even find the seams of things hidden carefully all these years.

"I feel certain," the Panditji said now, with some sanctimony, "that Jaya is amongst this group."

"You may be right, my dear," Ravi said, always comforting the Panditji but not fully believing—just in case they he had to agree with the Panditji on the opposite point, later on.

"Hmmph," the Panditji said. "We will see."

As the rains finally slowed into a mist and stopped, the night grew steamy hot. Then the mosquitos arose to call on those asleep and dreaming, collecting dues without prejudice from all who laid in the miasma of this ancient, humid town. All suffer the same pinpricks, all bleed the same red blood.

Mr. Kapadia, of the University in Varanasi, received Josh where he lived, in a bungalow adjoining the main campus. He was at the age where he was transitioning from old to elderly, probably in his mid-eighties, and he sat Josh down in his personal study, overflowing with books that covered his area of practice, sociology.

"Now, what is it you wish to learn? Your publisher in Delhi, they have a very good reputation," he said in a sophisticated accent.

Josh stumbled a bit, unsure of how to proceed with his two requests, but forged on. He confidently made his first request to borrow Mr. Kapadia's historical books for his research. Mr. Kapadia was hesitant, as some of these books had been in his family for generations. In the end, he offered a few books on loan, insisting on writing a promissory note on the spot, as he said, so he wouldn't forget.

"Now, Josh," he said. "What else do you want to learn?"

Josh sat in a comfortable faux-leather chair, clutching a packet of old books wrapped in a cast-off sari cloth for safe keeping. "You can tell?" he asked.

"Indeed, I can. I've been a lecturer, you know, a long time, Josh," Mr. Kapadia said. "In sociology, nonetheless. So I know a little bit about human behavior."

"You see, sir," Josh said. "Some friends and I, we are looking for some people in Varanasi. How to explain. They are connected, we think with the ghats. One ghat, in particular. But the thing is, these people, they would have been here a long time ago. I'm talking hundreds and hundreds of years ago."

Mr. Kapadia's smile slipped a bit. "Oh... I wish I could help you, Josh. But, you see, I've actually just shifted to Varanasi, from Lucknow, about ten years back. I know, for you, that probably sounds like a long time. But for the sort of people you are looking for, it would not be long enough. It's a shame. I don't think I would be much help."

"Josh, if you're going to see this Mrs. Kumar, I think I'd like to come with you," Jaya said first thing in the morning as they lay curled up in bed. The past week had been one of frustration. Josh had been down numerous dead ends. Similar to Mr. Kapadia, he'd met other kind, interested people willing to help him, but with no real ability to do so. The last name on Amrita's list, a Mr. Kumar, of the Institute of Hindu and Vedic Studies, was also a dead end, quite literally. When he'd called, Mr. Kumar's widow answered the phone. She explained, in smart, British-accented English, that though her husband, God rest his soul, had recently passed, from a long, sad disease which she required no special condolences for, she would be happy to meet Josh in his stead.

"It's an obligation, Jaya, nothing more. I don't think Mrs. Kumar will have anything. No one else did," Josh said. He hated this feeling of being stymied.

"I hope you're wrong," Jaya said. "For our sakes. I fear that the Panditji must be closer by now, since he has been probably looking for us."

Later that day, Mrs. Kumar received them in her late husband's study, a blue room with bookshelves cut into the limestone walls. She was dressed in a high-quality salwar kameez, fashionable despite her age and widowed status, which was not the norm in India. They continued in stilted, awkward small talk for forty-five minutes until Josh asked about the books for his Sanskrit-to-Russian translation project. On his request about someone who might know of a Kala Ghat sadhu, she had nothing to offer. And, as Josh had predicted, they were getting nowhere.

"But you expect me to know something about a sadhu? We are an intellectual family, I'm afraid. We do not have any ties to priests," Mrs. Kumar said. Her manners did not allow her to stop there.

"Tell me, dear," she said to Jaya. "How is it that you and your friend come to be here, anyway. You must pardon me for saying, but it is a bit unique, you know."

Jaya felt such relief to be in the presence of such a kind woman, who reminded her even a little of her Daadi Ma, though she was not "grandma-like" at all, and without realizing it, she spilled everything. How she had come to India due to her family and the ashram, and her family's land in Maalpur.

"Wait. You are from Maalpur?" Mrs. Kumar asked.

"Yes," Jaya nodded, "I'm originally from Maalpur—well, my family is."

"But I am from there, too!" Mrs. Kumar exclaimed. "I think, perhaps, I might know your family. Gupta, is it? Yes, I think I may know. And then, you must be there for the PKM Ashram. But you must tell me. Is this question you have, about this sadhu, related somehow to him, you know, the Panditji?" In her surprise, she got carried away, and let her reserve fall away.

"How did you know that this would be related to the Panditji?" Jaya said simply. "Actually, the thing is, something bad has happened with him."

"This doesn't surprise me, unfortunately, about the Panditji, but I've never told anyone about this. Are you sure you want to hear it?" Mrs. Kumar asked carefully.

"Yes, we do." Jaya leaned in closer to Josh and grabbed his hand. She looked expectantly at Mrs. Kumar.

"I always thought the Panditji was not what he seemed," Mrs. Kumar started, getting straight to the point, a very uncommon approach for most Indian women of her generation. "He taught, back then, a unique style of yoga. One time, I was about fifteen years old, and at his school during meditation, sitting with my eyes closed, in savasana. The Panditji told me, 'Now you must breathe, from deep in your soul.' I was a teenager, not accustomed to sitting still at all, you understand. As I sat there, my emotions changed. My whole being became filled with raw, elemental anger. I had never, in my life, experienced any type of anger like that. It was a consuming rage. The colors of purple and red and orange danced in front of my closed eyes. A strong headache pierced my skull, and I opened my eyes. The Panditji was staring at me, his eyes echoing the same, deep anger that I was feeling already. That was when I knew. He put that emotion in my mind. Never before had I experienced any anger like this, and never since. Not even after my dear Mr. Kumar passed away. How else would it come into my being, except through the yogi?

"I left the ashram that day, shaken by the experience, and after that, no matter how much my mother tried to induce me to return to the Panditji's ashram, to help with the local Shiva Moon Festival, I always refused. Ever since then, I knew, that place was not what it seemed. How could an ashram, run by a holy man, be filled with so much rage?"

"Perhaps, Mrs. Kumar, you were more right than you knew," Jaya said, feeling at ease enough to disclose everything. And she told her. About how the Panditji could bend the rules of life itself and about his book and about how some form of the Panditji had been alive for the past seven hundred years. When Jaya reached the part about the Panditji being alive continuously, Mrs. Kumar's tea cup fell out of her hands and split into two neat pieces on the floor.

"I believe you," Mrs. Kumar gasped, embarrassed over her clumsiness. "What is this world coming to anyway? Even the holy men are corrupt," she mused.

"Mrs. Kumar, do you, by chance, have any pictures of the Panditji?" Jaya asked, perking up with an idea. "You see, we need to test something. He looks about fifty years old right now. How old did he look when you were going to his ashram?"

"I guess he looked to be in his late twenties."

"So that would mean this all happened about sixty years ago, right? And yet, Panditji seems so much younger than sixty years of age. Mrs. Kumar, do you have a picture of the Panditji?"

In response, Mrs. Kumar called for a maid and asked her to bring the boxes of old pictures from the store room. She was quiet as she rummaged through the boxes, until she found the photo she wanted.

"See?" she said excitedly. "See this picture?" The image showed two teenage girls on each side of a yogi. "This was taken in Maalpur. At the PKM Ashram."

"But this picture isn't the Panditji," Jaya said with doubt. "That's definitely not him... Oh my GOD!" Jaya turned to Josh. "This means?"

Josh was smiling from ear to ear in self-satisfaction. "You know what this means. Between Mrs. Kumar's picture and your knowledge, together you have evidence of the link of one Panditji to the next."

"But how could we be certain?" Mrs. Kumar asked.

"The eyes," Jaya said. "The expression in those eyes are the same. And the rage. Mrs. Kumar, you said he filled you with rage and anger. Well, what he did to me was much, much worse. He tried to poison me, and I escaped, just barely. I'm sorry to tell you, but he is right now hunting me in Varanasi, as we speak. This has to be the same person. He just took a break, in between lives, for about a decade or so."

"Well, now that you say it, your theory might have some merit. Because you are confirming for me, about my own experiences, and dear, I'm so sorry to hear of yours. Anyway, you see after marrying my dear Mr. Kumar, I left Maalpur for my new in-laws' hometown. I heard some time later that the ashram fell into disrepair, and then a family, your family, Jaya, I would think, moved in."

They all sat in tense silence, letting the gravity of this meeting sink in. Just like that, the series of disconnected threads were interweaving themselves into a thick twine, forming a rope that tied one part of the present to a recent part of the past: Jaya's near-death experience and Panditji's influence on Mrs. Kumar as a young woman.

CHAPTER THIRTEEN

Penitents and Seekers

Once Ravi set his mind to it, it took hardly half a day to find them. He simply walked down to the main auto-rickshaw area where the drivers hung out, picked the first driver he saw, handed him a twenty rupee note, and firmly told him he needed to get a special medicine from the Panditji to an Australian film star. The driver, a glassy-eyed young man with a face full of teenage acne and perhaps under the influence of bhang, barely even nodded. He enthusiastically pulled out into the traffic as if he knew where to go.

As it turned out, it was no straight route. The auto rickshaw sputtered along at barely 10 k.p.h., the driver stopping frequently and leaning halfway out of the cab to proposition passersby on the whereabouts of one Australian film star. Most of those who were accosted looked at the driver with some disdain. After three such encounters, the young man, sensing his customer was getting frustrated, made a beeline to a roadside cafeteria that doubled as a mechanic shop. Generally, he found customers were less annoyed after they had a cold drink. After all, what was the hurry? The more time to be entertained by this self-important holy man, and his potentially illegal "medicine" for the Australian film star. The driver was no newbie. He knew this town brought the crazies.

At the roadside cafeteria, a mechanic came out to greet them. He was heavyset and hairy. "Australian phfilm star? Ohhhhh haan, yes, it is Jeep. I fix! He has six Jeeps. Big Jeeps. He is put up in the old Nawab's house," the mechanic said.

"How to get?" the driver inquired, splaying out his hand and nodding at the same time.

"How to?" the mechanic said, scratching his hair with a grease-caked fingernail, trying to think of how to provide directions to a place he just knew by heart. "Down this way," here he pointed straight ahead, "marble white roof. Five minutes. Can't miss. Tell him, to bring his big Jeep to see me, Kamlesh," the mechanic finished, smiling awkwardly. Apparently, this Australian film star had left an impression on him.

"Okay, okay," the driver said, nodding, hopping with vigor back into his seat to replay what he'd learned to Ravi.

Still, they would have driven right past the Nawab's place had it not been for Ravi. The driver, none too stable, was relishing these empty streets, topping out at 25 k.p.h. and humming a rap song from a Hindi movie, which he punctuated by shouting the chorus line.

"Peeyuu peeyuu," he sang, while pretending to shoot a fake gun and imagining the heroine shaking her hips with the rhythm.

"Here!" Ravi shouted, spotting the house.

"Oh yes, YES, of course. Sir. This here? This is Nawab's house. Here is your Australian phfilm star," the driver said with a rich confidence completely at odds with his total inability to find the joint in the first place.

"Okay, stop now. I will get out here," Ravi said, rolling his eyes, wanting to disembark before they got to the main gate. Better to go in the side door, than the front, he thought.

"Sir? No, I take you in the house. Surely. You just wait, I will get the gate guard. Maybe I will ask for autograph, too, from phfilm star's girlfriend!" the driver said.

"No, no. That will not be necessary. I insist!" Sensing the driver wasn't going to easily give up this opportunity for any reason, Ravi waited until the rickshaw driver had slowed down to a reasonable speed, then hopped out, throwing him another twenty rupee note for good measure.

"Hey, man!" the driver said, still coasting while reaching over to pocket the note. "Hey!" Then he remembered he was talking to a holy man, in a pristine white outfit. He'd lived in Varanasi long enough to know those guys had the power to bless or curse him. And so he shrugged, and still coasting, lit the last centimeter of an already-smoked cigarette, and put his foot down on the pedal and let it rip. With any luck he'd remember this film star's house for future profit. It wasn't a bad day, after all.

Ten types of fruit juice were laid out on Dan's brunch table. They were there for a celebration, for Mrs. Kumar had finally come through with a lead.

About those juices. There was the standard-issue orange juice, of course, and a sweet, tart apple, and a buttery papaya, and a sour mango hailing from Mumbai, and a blackberry concoction made of different blue-hued berries, and the juice of three kiwi fruits mixed with sugar, and a cucumber-lime spritz, and a honeydew—which if one were being honest was slightly too bitter—and a cane sugar juice, popular in these parts for its hydrating powers, and the tenth, a metabolism-inducing pineapple mixed with turmeric.

"So we're all going, right?" Dan asked Josh. True to form, heedless of the time of day, he was busy mixing a flask of dubiously provenanced grain alcohol into one of the juices. Today he wore an ensemble of turquoise blue khakis and a salmon pink fishing vest, which he paired with a turquoise headband and white plastic sunglasses.

"Actually, um, she said just Jaya and me."

"Purpose?" Dan quizzed.

Jaya turned expectedly as well.

"We're to meet someone she thinks we should meet," Josh replied.

"Now who could that be?" Nisha inquired.

"Her brother?" said Jaya, surprising herself with her outburst.

"The Panditji!" whooped Dan's assistant.

"A former yoga student?" Nisha added.

"Guys, guys, you have it all wrong," Josh said. "Ten bucks. It's one of those touts from the ghats."

"You all had better take a recorder, okay, yeah? Maybe, you know, we'll get some good audio out of it," Dan said, hiding his disappointment that he could not go with them. "When is it, again, that you're going?"

"Oh, she said to come, tomorrow at 10 a.m.," Josh said, this last piece directed at Jaya.

"Tomorrow it is then," Jaya said, with some finality.

"You both must come inside now. I have a Pujari, a priest, here who is going to talk with you." Mrs. Kumar was animated and energetic when Jaya and Josh came to call. This new challenge had cut through the depression of recent widowhood and brought back some of her natural élan. For that, she was grateful.

For their part, Jaya and Josh agreed on the way over to strive for a level of polite maturity, hoping to retain some semblance of reason, and to let what was to come, come. The temptation to dramatize was high, especially with Dan Katt's backstage machinations, and they each at this moment felt the keen desire to resist the puppet master's call. And anyway, the mystery guest was soon enough revealed.

In Mrs. Kumar's study sat a disheveled older man, dressed in an all-white ensemble of a T-shirt and a loose cotton dhoti, thin and spare, with white greasy hair and the unexpected complexion of a northern European. He peered at them through coke-bottle glasses.

"This is our family Pujari. He has come," Mrs. Kumar paused and took a deep breath, "he has come from Maalpur."

"Namaste, Pujariji," Jaya said. Josh bowed his head as well, following her lead. He was fiddling a bit, to get the recorder going, as Dan Katt had expressly ordered.

"After all," Mrs. Kumar began, "this is something from Maalpur, I said. And Pujari is the oldest person I know from that place. He has lived many lives, you could say, in a way." She had an intellectual's flair for the dramatic.

"You are wondering, how did I find this person?" Mrs. Kumar said quietly. "This priest has been a close family friend for years, and I asked him, point blank, about this Panditji business that you both explained. And he said yes, there was a ritual that people talked about, back when he was a youth."

Taking his cue from Mrs. Kumar, the Pujari jumped in. "Friends," he began. He had a surprisingly strong voice, delivered in a thick accent with some softness at the edges due to his missing teeth. "Friends, you want to know moksha chakra, the dark pooja that joins the soul to consciousness forever."

"But how?" Jaya gulped, choking and coughing in her surprise. To hear another person give form to the contours of what she had learned, she felt this moment could not be real. It was adding confirmation to the things she had accepted in a kind of perpetual motion of disbelief.

"You must tell me, child, about yourself," the Pujari said firmly.

And so, Jaya told him. She told him her name, Jaya Gupta, and of her family, the Guptas of Maalpur, and how they had lived there until they had sold off the land. She mentioned her father and mother and Daadi Ma. How she had been raised with a good education, how she had spent some time away from home at the ashram. These were standard Indian appeals—that vouched that the one speaking was a good, humble, and decent person who had done all the right things and who deserved, due to various hardships, to be given consideration for what they were asking from this person.

The Pujari's hands were clasped, and he was smiling beatifically, brimming with pride to see a prodigal daughter return to the Motherland with the proper values.

Jaya continued. "My grandmother determined I must go to Maalpur, in order to see our land and to stay connected with our culture. Now it is a yoga ashram, so there I went, and stayed with Panditji Kaaju Maharaj and went to his school for the past few months. There is where I, through an accident, came upon a diary." She paused and nodded to Josh, who pulled out the book from his backpack.

The Pujari strained through his glasses. "May I?" he asked.

"This diary, Pujari, this was the Panditji's. Imagine, I could hardly believe it, but it started over seven hundred years ago. And then he confronted me, when he thought I had found his diary, and he tried to poison me. It was only through some luck that I even escaped and am here. And, I don't know what else to say," she looked down, trying to control the anger coursing through her anew. Josh tensed on the sofa with her, putting his hand quietly on her elbow to steady her.

"I see," the Pujari said, shifting a little in his seat, noticing this interpersonal reaction between her and Josh. "Yes, I see.

Jayaji, you must know, that we Hindus are not so obsessed with good and evil. We must come to terms and live the righteous path. But this Panditji, this thing he has done, it is a ritual impurity that is against all correct forms of nature. Please, let me explain. You see, this Kala Ghat of which you are speaking, in Varanasi, when I was a youth, this place existed, and there was a disreputable sadhu and he used to offer this moksha chakra ritual, where the owner would be joined to the soul and consciousness for eternity. This was eternal consciousness, you know, meaning to cheat on the path of the soul's continual journey through multiple lives toward learning and then to nirvana and oneness with God. Quite dangerous, against all nature. Even I was trained in this technique, yes."

Mrs. Kumar gasped and shook her head. Josh startled. Jaya looked sharply at him.

The Pujari shrugged, revealing a glimpse of the carefree man he must have been in his youth. "I was young—a young man, curious. The sadhu made this seem simple. He said, if I were a good person, then why not be good forever, why not spread this goodness through multiple lives, and help other people. It was so simple. I was convinced. I was excited, but, oh, my parents heard of this, and they forbid me from ever going to this ghat again. They explained that not everyone was good. That there would be some who might use this ritual for evil purposes. Later, when I was more mature, I saw that they were right, and that I had almost been seduced by the promise of something that seemed incredible, for what purposes and to what effect I still cannot know. I'm sorry to say, but the Panditji can hardly be the only one who has taken this ritual. There are surely to be more men like him, who were convinced. And I do hope that most who did this were good people. But what about those who did not have a similar morality?

"Now that I see your intentions are pure, that you are of strong character and good heart, that you believe in the Hindu ideals, as do you," he nodded at Josh, "even though you are not Indian, I see you have respect for our faith and for our traditions. This matters. Now I understand the problem. You are not interested in taking the moksha chakra. I am most relieved, actually. I did not think, after you had explained yourselves, that you would be of the sort looking to engage in these dark arts. But, one can never be too sure. But yes," he said, as he stroked his chin, "I see now that no, you are not interested in the moksha chakra. Actually, you are interested in *undoing* this procedure."

He paused.

Jaya nodded. "Yes, that's right. That's exactly right." She felt, for the first time, as if she might be rid of this terrible curse that pressed down on her forehead constantly, the new reality that she could hardly believe was hers. What the Pujari said made total sense. If the soul had been joined to the consciousness, then surely it must be and could be severed as well. That was the only way to remove the Panditji from his power.

Josh put his hand on her back, in solidarity. Mrs. Kumar stared into the wall, her expression one of deep emotion, but difficult to place.

"That is not a ritual, sadly, that I know of, nor that I know how to undertake," said the Pujari, holding out his hands. Jaya's face fell. "I am an old man, and it pains me to see the Hindu culture defiled like this, and I have nothing to fear from the Panditji or his people, nor from death itself, which would be a welcome relief when my time comes and takes me from the misery of this human condition. We all must play our part." He nodded sadly and kindly, and sat quite still while he waited for all of this to sink in, a man wiser even than his advanced years.

The room's energies dissipated with everyone lost in their own thoughts. A radio played somewhere on a neighbor's property, wafting tunes from a 1970s-era movie, a high-pitched woman's voice leading the lilting vocals. The light gauze curtains fluttered in the short breeze. The overhead fan beat rhythmically on an oscillating tilt. Somewhere, a clock ticked loudly. Josh clicked his voice recorder off. Whatever it was that each participant had wanted from this meeting had certainly been received.

Dan Katt was overcome with the hyperactive imaginings of a creative soul given too much stimulus. For the first time in three years of wandering the world documenting the weird for his TV show, he had found a place to dwell. His meeting Jaya and Josh, and their story, had fired off so many ideas in his brain that he could hardly control them. Of course, there could be no question that he would find and meet the Panditji.

Oh, he had a good idea of who the Panditji was and how he looked, both from Jaya's descriptions and what his assistants found online. He saw in his mind's eye how the Panditji would sit in front of the camera, resplendent, a corrupt villain in his shiny, white silk kurta pajama and dark kohl eyeliner and, the pièce de résistance, a wholly unnecessary white turban with a single diamond in its center.

Would the Panditji submit to an interview, however provocative it may be? Of course, this must happen. In addition to the behind-the-scenes exposé featuring Jaya and Josh, and their back story. Romantic. Oh, that alone could fetch an action romance spin-off series, Dan reckoned.

But Dan started to think bigger as he sipped on a gin and tonic, sniffing the herbal smell of the sprig of rosemary swirling inside. This was so much more than a few TV shows and B-list movies. Dan dreamed of billion-dollar, mega-hit movies.

Pulsing action movies, with him in the starring role, wearing an impossibly hirsute costume wig, his muscles bulging, rippling, as he saved a woman from the clutches of the evil Panditji. He imagined the red carpets, all the right international film festivals. The inevitable Oscar buzz. This movie would have a real, authentic villain at the center—scarier than anything fiction could create—and it would set the world afire.

This would be just the thing, Dan thought, a new form of entertainment: blending real and action. No more computer-generated animation, no more storybook villains and heroes; this was the real deal, raw as a wound and hypnotic like a mother fucker. He would retire in five years, a media mogul, bigger than all the other bigs, on his own island in an as-yet undiscovered part of the ocean off his beloved Australia, to live life exactly as he chose. If, and this was a big *if*, he chose right, just now. Dan swirled his glass and sucked down the last of the gin, blinking when his gaze fixed finally on something into the distance.

"Could you stop here?" Josh asked the driver as the car entered the main gates of Dan's compound. Jaya was silent, absorbing what they had learned from the Pujari.

Josh flipped his dark curly hair and stretched his arms up above his head as he got out of the car.

"Come with me," he said to Jaya, grabbing her hand and pulling her out, too. He threw an arm around her, pushing her along as they walked off.

"Where are we going?" Jaya asked. They were trundling toward the gardens. Their light sandals smacked the muddy grass.

"Let's find a spot to sit and think," Josh said.

They found a marble fountain inside a small garden, walled off by bamboo trees. Inside the cove, it was cool, as the tall cylindrical bamboos reached up to the sky, shielding the sun.

"What's on your mind, Jaya?" Josh asked as they sat on a bench in the corner. He held her hand, massaging it.

"I... don't know. I'm overwhelmed, I guess. Really, after talking to the Pujari, it seems that the Panditji, the moksha chakra ceremony, it's all real. I didn't dream it. How can this be happening?" Jaya shook her head, and her eyes teared up. "I'm living in a nightmare."

"No, Jaya, no, you're not." Josh pushed her hair out of her face. "Okay, maybe this is a nightmare, this Panditji and what he tried to do to you. But, Jaya, we found each other. You're one of the most special people I've ever met." Josh's eyes were darker than they'd ever been, intense, and focused on her.

Tears welling up in Jaya's eyes spilled over. It was all too much emotion. The relief of knowing she wasn't alone in her knowledge of the Panditji's sins. And now, Josh. For so long, she'd been looking for someone to share reality with. And here was Josh, and he was here.

"Why are you crying?"

"I'm just... relieved, happy... I'm happy that you and I met."

And before Josh could stop himself, he leaned over and kissed her passionately, with all that he had felt about her since the moment he met her. The emotions rose, and they were too much for both. In the excitement of all that had happened, the running about, the constant physical danger, they had found comfort in each other. But now, with recourse in sight, they felt truly safe for the first time, and Jaya and Josh made love in the shade of the bamboo trees.

"Won't someone see us?" Jaya asked nervously, but with a smile.

"Sshh, don't worry. Pretty sure Dan Katt's staff sees this kind of stuff all the time," Josh said with a chuckle.

Afterwards, as they pulled their clothes back on, Jaya smiled and laughed to herself. "Of course," she muttered.

"Of course what?" Josh said, feeling proud of himself, kissing her on the forehead.

"I just mean, of course. All those guys I dated in New York who hardly had time to meet for coffee every few months. And you, we meet on the plane, we hang out in Goa, you help me with all of this, take a break from your job, and it's easy. It makes sense."

"I know what you mean," Josh said slowly. "I left a girlfriend behind in New York. No, don't worry, we broke up. It would've been too hard to continue long distance. But that's the thing, Jaya. It was too hard. And this? With you? It's just simple."

On the other side of Dan's compound, unbeknown to Josh and Jaya on their morning adventures, disaster was looming. Ravi, who had been nosing about the place after his morning rickshaw ride, fell out of a tree. Not just any tree. A tree of the fig family bordering the Nawab's rented palatial estate.

Ravi had spent a good chunk of an hour lurking around the property, trying to find a vantage point from which to see what was going on inside. He'd tried jumping up and down to see over the hedges. He'd tried fashioning a stool to lift himself. When that failed, he climbed a gnarled tree. The too short, too thin branches supported his weight for about three minutes, until they did not. He fell from a short height into the hedge row that he'd been seeking to breach. At first, he'd rolled about, comically, on top, the branches pricking him through his fine cotton day clothes. By then, Dan's staff had heard the commotion, and the Butler came running with the gardener in tow. The gardener, Maali, a prima donna at the best of times, who was constantly getting into daily tiffs with the Butler, was directed to take charge. Maali poked at Ravi with the handle of a long broom, as if the intruder were a rabid squirrel, to bring him down. The Butler's strong hands broke his fall.

"Who are you? What is this mischief? Why are you here?" the Butler demanded. His stern manner was softened after one look at Ravi's appearance: clean cut, well-dressed and attractive. It seemed this might be a casual mistake.

Ravi kept his eyes focused on the house, refusing to speak, still lying on the ground, wondering if he'd broken any bones. Without the Panditji, he felt like a puppet without its strings. For so long, he had been with him. What should his next move be? Closing his eyes, he took a deep breath, to calm himself. The outside world it was an illusion, a maya. He would remain in internal peace. He stiffened and lay silent while the world around him moved.

On their self-satisfied walk back through the large, grassy expanse to the main house, Jaya and Josh discussed the Pujari and his knowledge of the moksha chakra.

"To think, Josh, to think this is real. This is real. That crazy book. The Panditji. His past lives. It's actually real," Jaya said.

"Do you think he'll find the reversing ceremony, the one to undo the moksha chakra?" Josh said, as they hopped up the steps. "I for one am skeptical that it would be possible."

Jaya frowned and raised her hand to shield her eyes as she peered up to the marble veranda, where there was an inert figure of a man in all-white clothing and his arms bound behind his back. Her heart thumped as she realized the figure looked familiar. Closer now, she saw that it was Ravi, the man who had most recently tried to kill her and leave her for dead. She became utterly still, fear coursing through her.

"Josh," she said, her voice neutral. "Please don't be alarmed, or make any noises."

Noting her pale expression, Josh said nothing, but nodded and followed her. She was tiptoeing, trying to make herself invisible as they went into the house.

"Josh!" she whispered, pointing towards the veranda. "*That* is Ravi. The Panditji's *Ravi*. The man who tried to kill me."

"What?!"

"Get Dan and the Butler and anyone else you can think of. We've got a crisis on our hands!"

Her head whirled. Something bilious rose up inside her, something full of pepper and vim, mean and punitive. At least now she was in control. She had Josh. And she was at Dan's house. On his turf, she had power. Wouldn't it be interesting to know how it was that Ravi, the Panditji's aider and abettor, had landed like a wounded bird, tied up on Dan's front doorstep?

She thought of all the people who had been cheated out of their lives too early, one of whom might have been her. And for what reason? For what purpose, except to allow Ravi and the Panditji to continue living another cycle of their borrowed lives. She thought of all that had been taken from her family, and the land that was no longer theirs. Weighing on her mind again was the depravity of those who would seek to retard the laws of humanity; to hijack the progress of the wheel of life for their own ends; and to do so in the name of a religion that she believed in. She thought of the legions of yoga students, all taught something they believed to be good and just, not knowing what original sins lied within, that they unconsciously accepted and perpetuated. It was what the Panditji had sowed, a seed of evil, that spread through centuries. And then, perhaps because her mind could not process the magnitude of so much wickedness, and because she was feeling the bloom of love she had always hoped she deserved, her whole being short-circuited and she laughed out loud—a hard, cynical laugh.

She laughed to herself, in the room alone, as Dan and his coterie and Josh came rushing back, with concerned looks on their faces. When they showed her Ravi's supine form up close, Jaya stiffened. She locked her knees, sucked in her lower belly, and set her shoulders back. She looked with perfect clarity at Dan and Josh and Nisha, her eyes crystal green, shining with resolve. Whatever happened, wherever the Panditji might be—

which wasn't likely to be far—she would show no mercy. *No,* she corrected herself, *together, they would show no mercy.*

Relief finally crashed through Jaya, eliciting tears.

"Jaya?" Josh said, worried. "What's wrong? Why are you crying?"

"It's nothing," she said, smiling and wiping her eyes. "It's just, I feel so lucky. To have you, and all of you guys. To be here. To be safe."

Josh said nothing, just scooped her up in his arms, holding her tight. He had a brooding look on his face as he looked up at the others. "We have to call the police."

He noticed Dan filming the two of them and shouted, "I said RIGHT NOW, Dan! You can do your shoot later."

The Butler heard the seriousness in Josh's voice and rushed to the front gate, where he let out a loud double whistle. In less than a few minutes, a beat cop at the end of the block was alerted, and down the street came the sounds of a siren and a jeep headed straight for Dan's house.

Out of the open-topped jeep came a heavyset cop in a beige uniform. He huffed to the front steps as a younger, thinner underling ran up and stood behind him.

"What is the meaning of this?!" the Inspectorji demanded loudly, adjusting his belt buckle angrily and waving his cap in his hand.

"This man is harassing my guests! I am an international movie star! This will not stand!" Dan shouted back, sunglasses on, stance aggressive.

The Inspectorji, recognizing a fellow screamer in Dan, stepped up to the plate. "You!" he yelled in the general direction of his second in command. "This situation will be assessed in the proper manner. Ashish—bring him to the station. Let us go!" He replaced his cap smartly on his head, nodded at Dan, and popped back up into the jeep, surprisingly gracefully for being so overstuffed in his suit. Off Ravi went.

The Panditji broke his daily fast with a richer than normal meal, which the restaurant at his guesthouse prepared to commemorate the auspicious nighttime birth of Vishnu's sixth avatar. He closed his eyes as he took in each bite of the buttery flatbread, the special mashed pumpkin dish, and a potato, pea and tomato-broth dish, washing it all down with cool water from a stainless-steel mug.

Though the food was heavenly, he could not take full pleasure in his meal as a wave of anger and hate flooded through his system. Ravi was not here, which was unlike him. There could be only one reason. Jaya. One way or another, he thought, it must be her fault. His Ravi had been with him, literally, for centuries.

How dare this Jaya gain acceptance to his ashram? How dare she steal his secrets, then casually reveal them despite not understanding them fully? What sort of strength did she possess to be able to run away from him? She was no special human. During yoga class, as he recalled, she was utterly mediocre. She complained faster than most when certain positions led to pain. She could not perform the more complicated arm lifts. She was less limber than her peers. Eager to please, overly optimistic, and thoroughly corruptible she was, as many in her situation were. And yet, she did resist. She did rise up and flee when faced with death. For the Panditji, this was new territory. No one ever ran. New, he scoffed to himself, after so many hundreds of years. This was the first time that he must contemplate some other way to silence a foe.

Almost casually, he crooked his finger, sending the restaurant's one waiter rushing over.

"Sir?"

"Boy, find me the local policeman. Here." He handed him a 100 rupee note. "Bring him here."

"Sir?"

"That's not all. Also, bring me your local priest, the one who works at the temple around the corner."

"Sir? But he is busy with the festival today."

"Oh, here," the Panditji said, handing the boy two more 100 rupee notes. "You give one to the policeman and two to the priest."

"Sir?"

"Now, boy. Go now. And don't come back until you have them. And if you do, perhaps I give you some rupees too, for your troubles."

Shrugging, the boy jogged his lanky self and thick black plastic sandals out onto the street.

"Hey!" said the cook from his perch at the front of the restaurant. "Who's going to serve these people? Me?"

The Panditji ignored him, satisfied, and took another large helping of food. The outlines of a plan were taking shape. Ravi would be found. Jaya would be controlled. Since she wanted to live so badly, she could live forever. But, he thought, dispassionately, she would never be free. He'd see to that.

CHAPTER FOURTEEN

Concerned Parties

I f Dan was surprised to see Mrs. Kumar driving up to his house, he didn't show it. The car was a boxy white sedan of Indian make.

"I shall get straight to the point," Mrs. Kumar said, getting out of the car and meeting eyes with Jaya, then Josh, then Dan. She was dressed impeccably, as always, in a smart navy day salwar kameez, and flanked by two guests.

"The Pujari and his colleague, Srikanth," she turned and nodded in their direction, "are aware of some rituals we must perform." Her English was crisp, and she tipped her chin up as she spoke, ever the brave widow. "Tonight."

What Mrs. Kumar then recounted would be remembered for many years to come. The Butler led the party to an elegant, red-upholstered room with red leather couches and red carpets and red bookshelves. The Nawab, from whom Dan was renting this house, had made this his personal sitting room when he had lived here, so its regal nature was appropriate. The ceiling fans churned, as did the standing oscillating fans stationed in every corner, the combined effect of which imparted to the room a low and continuous hum. The fireplace, incongruous in the heat of India, sat magnanimously, unused, along one wall. A framed painting of a seventeenth-century rajah on a tiger hunt hung above the fireplace, tying the room together.

Given the urgency of Mrs. Kumar's comment earlier, few pleasantries were exchanged amongst the group as Dan and Nisha, Josh and Jaya, the Pujari, Mrs. Kumar and their friend assembled themselves on the chairs and couches. The usual small talk was skipped. The introductions were passed over. Even the Butler, fascinated by what was to come, forgot to signal his assistant Butler for orange sherbets and salty munchies. So the guests went thirsty, and snackless, as the widow brought them up to speed on what her priestly friends had uncovered.

"Perhaps I should ask the obvious question," Josh began, leaning forward, his dark curly hair falling into his eyes, his hands clasped in a knot on his bare knees. "Why tonight?"

Next to him, Jaya held her breath.

"Well, son," the elderly Pujari began, "yes, that is a very good question. It is having a very simple answer." He paused and looked around the room with his thick glasses. He took a deep breath, as if steeling himself for what would come next, noting the anxious, youthful faces staring back at him. "Because tonight is first night of new moon. And this pooja that we are to be suggesting, it is best to be performed in new moon time. This is, Srikanth, say hello"—Srikanth raised his hands in namaste— "he is just in town, you see? For this week, for some special training, and then he must go back to his home village where his mother is having to be in the hospital for some heart conditions. So you see, this is the best most auspicious time."

"Hello," Srikanth said in a thick accent of a sort Jaya had not yet heard. He was thin and spotless, wearing a crisp tan pajama suit. Overall, he gave the impression of someone fastidious in his appearance and also deeply insecure, a hard-worker who watched others closely to see how he must get by. "Please tell them," he said to the Pujari, before turning to everyone else. "Begging your pardon, but I will ask Pujari to explain in English, as mine is less expertise." His eyes sparkled black, but he remained a man of few words, dazzled a bit by these foreigners and self-conscious. He did not often meet with people from other countries, let alone native English speakers.

"See here," the Pujari said, taking over, "this moksha chakra business that you have reminded me of, that I considered to do so many years ago, that it seems this corrupt yoga man has undergone." The Pujari paused, reached down almost habitually for a glass of water, but not feeling anything, shrugged and continued, "Well, see, this ritual which Srikanth is knowing, it could be reducing its potentials."

"Reducing its potentials?" Jaya echoed slowly, shaking her head. A part of her was frustrated, because she thought somehow with Ravi in jail, that they might be done. Wishful thinking, she knew now.

"See," said the Pujari in his deep, shaky voice. "This is not 100 percent like the science." He held up a hand, to emphasize the halting nature of this endeavor. "Nothing is to be certain. As you must know. Life is not certain. This young man, Srikanth," here he nodded, "he has a specialty in performing birth rites. He is doing many rites for young mothers and newborn children, to make the insurance that they are coming into this world fully whole." Srikanth sat next to them silently, nodding vigorously. The Pujari continued, "Whole you see—with no imperfections—of mind or body or soul. One must, you see, attach a soul and a body together, bind them as one, so that whenever the child is born, then he is fully connected to the body of this newborn baby. This must be our answer." The Pujari looked around the room confidently, as if the matter were settled.

"I'm not sure I understand, sir," Jaya said, shaking her head, grabbing a hold of Josh's hand that was next to her. "How would this be helpful?" Her face was full of doubt. She didn't want to have hope.

"I have to say, in all my readings, nothing like this has ever surfaced," Josh noted. "I've read through hundreds of old Sanskrit texts, looking for connections to Russian. Vedic rituals. Horse sacrifices. Prayers to rain gods. Requests for thunder. Even approaches to manage the dead. But this one, ah, I have to say this is the first time I've heard of any ritual or need for anything remotely like this, but—"

"But just hold on now," Dan said, cutting him off and leaning forward, "this ritual, whatever it is? I can use this. For my show. Let's hear more, okay, I'm liking the sound of it."

"You see, you see," the Pujari said, continuing with a broad smile, "the moksha chakra, it is designed to make a soul to travel with a connected consciousness forever. This is correct, yes? Not a natural path. So you see, this ceremony, the one for the newborn, is designed actually to ensure that the nature is happening, that the newborn is taking the new soul to this body. This is why many superstitious people, they do not wish to cheat their karma—you live full life and gain the learnings owed in this life, so that the soul can travel closer toward the final state of nirvana. That is to say, it, meaning this ritual, most likely breaks the connection of the soul to some other past life or other consciousness; it is designed to ensure that the soul comes to the body pure. This is not a very common ritual, mind you. Srikanth, actually only, I am finding now because he is doing this ritual in the remote part of India where he is from, where there is much fear of children not being born fully formed."

Dan was not quite believing his luck. "I gotta say, this is going to be the best episode, like ever, in the history of TV. We have got to do this. We have to. A real-life priest performing this ceremony!" At the best of times Dan was able to embellish anything into an outrageous, amazing, life-altering experience. But this, this was next level.

"I see," Jaya said, ignoring Dan's enthusiastic pronouncements, "so it stands to reason that if a soul can be attached fully to a body, then it would weaken the connection to a prior consciousness. Is that it? That's the idea?"

"Precisely! If you can loosen the Panditji's connection to his prior lives, we can hope to break the link entirely," Mrs. Kumar said, jumping in. "But you have to understand," she added, "this is all theory. Never has this been tested. I hope it will be enough. This Panditji, he is an abomination. Jaya, you and I, we have a connection to him, through Maalpur. We have a responsibility to change his course."

"But how? How can we know it will work?" Jaya asked.

"Test it. Of course," Nisha said, shaking her head, realizing that, to Mrs. Kumar's point, they would have to test the theory.

"That is right, my dear," Mrs. Kumar said, warily. "The only way to see if this could work, you would need someone to perform the ritual upon." She gulped, then added tentatively,

"That's why we wanted to ask you dears, is the Panditji available?"

"Leave it to me, sirs."

They all looked up. The Butler was standing at the edge of the room, listening to it all.

"It is but the work of an afternoon to break Mr. Ravi out of jail," he said. "Simply give me the permissions and funding to go to the police. I will take care of it. He is not, of course, the Panditji, but surely for a test, he will suffice?"

"Are you sure this will work?" Josh asked.

"This is the best we can do. I think we must try," Mrs. Kumar said simply, refolding her starched body-length scarf. She traced a crease down from her mid-thigh to her knee, pausing to look up at Jaya, and added, "We women of Maalpur, Jaya, like your grandmother, and you now, despite your experiences in the ashram, we must try. That is why I am here, despite all of the trouble and hassle. I would prefer, you know, to just mourn my husband in peace. But I cannot. We must do something. And, Jaya, I'm sorry to say, you too must do your part."

At the central Varanasi police station, Inspector Naik had a surprisingly busy morning, all related to the man he'd picked up yesterday, this clean-cut yogi named Ravi from some northern town, who was sitting quietly in a cell down the hall.

The Butler, with Jaya in tow, had been the first to arrive to make his case. As a "concerned party" they stated flatly their desire on the part of his esteemed patron to ensure that the prisoner was not released upon any circumstance.

"Well, now," the Inspectorji said, sitting back in his chair and folding his hands over his large belly, "the law is the law, as you know. We can hold him twenty-four hours. Which will soon be up. As it was, he has not stolen anything, nor done much more than trespass. What reason do you have, sirs, to ask for this continuance?" The Inspectorji tilted his head, challenging them to a response.

Jaya looked around the room, painted all green, and leaned against the Inspectorji's large desk stacked with piles of papers. "Well, this man is known to us. He tried to kidnap me. We cannot allow him to walk free. My name is Jaya Gupta, and this is my friend's butler, and it was only through the grace of God that we were able to capture him when he landed upon the property of Dan Katt, international film star."

"Was a police report filed about this kidnapping? Where you were kidnapped?" the Inspectorji inquired, propping his thick finger against his drooping chin.

"Well, no, there's no police report, but..." Jaya replied helplessly.

The Inspectorji sighed. Certainly, he could let the prisoner go and wash his hands of this situation, but his experience told him that if the prisoner was important enough for someone to come inquiring about him, then it was worth finding out why. "What is it that you want? Jayaji? Butler*ji*," he said, emphasizing the "ji" honorific in a sarcastic way, implying the Butler's comparatively lower station in life.

The Butler ignored this. "We would like for this man to be released back to Dan Katt's compound, into our custody. We will question him, about this other matter, and then if his answers are sufficient, release him."

"Oho! So you are to play the law, is it? After all, you sent him here, did you not?" the Inspectorji said.

"This person, Inspectorji, you do not know what fire you are playing with," Jaya put in. "Does he look clean? Does he look respectable? He is not. He is part of a multigenerational crime that is so grave I cannot begin to tell you. You would not want to know."

"Perhaps I do, perhaps I don't." The Inspectorji stared at the clock ticking on his wall, to indicate that they were out of time.

The Butler got the hint, silently reached down to the floor to grab an expensive leather satchel, and put it on the table. Jaya closed her eyes, unable to believe that she was party to something like this. *Of course, Dan thought of everything,* she thought. The Inspectorji unzipped the bag and peeked in. It was filled with stacks of 100-rupee notes.

"What will you do to this prisoner? I should not like anything untoward to happen to him."

"Nothing worse than what he has done to others, including me," Jaya said quietly.

"I should like," here the Inspectorji cursed at himself for getting overinvolved, "to supervise the prisoner's remanding to the Dan Katt household. To ensure, of course, that nothing overmuch bad happens to him."

"Of course, sir. Of course," the Butler responded. Jaya nodded.

But the Inspectorji was not paying attention. He had taken the bills out of the bag and was counting them with his thick fingers. "Go on home, Jayaji, Butlerji," he said, not looking up. "Go on home now, and tell your friends that I will bring the prisoner to the house at 5pm sharp today. Not like Indian time, okay? European time, like you international types. I will bring two guards to ensure that the prisoner is not ill-treated."

"Actually," Jaya said, interrupting him, "we will need Ravi to be transported to a different location. A ghat on the banks of the Ganges. It is called the Kala Ghat."

"Sure, sure, wherever you wish. But mind, you chaps will have two more days, that is, forty-eight hours, to be with the prisoner. After this, he will be set free. Oh, and ensure you provide one more of these," he patted the leather satchel on the desk, "upon my arrival at this place. I have two sons, dear colleagues. They could use a fine bag such as this to carry to their fancy private schools. And the cash to go with it, of course, for their tuition. If your Dan Katt is the big star he says he is? Now go."

As Jaya and the Butler stood to leave, the Inspectorji yelled for the tea boy to bring his second cup of morning tea.

An hour later, the Butler was at the Kala Ghat to check up on the gardener, Maali, who had been dispatched to set up an area for tonight's impromptu rituals. Maali was looking distastefully around at the broken stone steps and pavilion, and the anemic grass growth.

"Begging your pardon, sir, but why such need to set up ritual pooja here in this place? Actually, I think we can find much nicer accommodations for our filmi star and his friends. I look, yes?" said Maali. He attempted to explain to the Butler that, why, just last month, had he not been commissioned to do the flowers for a large society wedding in Varanasi? Had the bride and her flower garlands not looked elegant, despite her general homeliness? This here? This was a fool's errand. How could one be beautifying a rundown ghat like this?

The Butler rolled his eyes and sensed a flare-up coming. "Do keep your unnecessary opinions to yourself today," he replied haughtily. "We do not have time today of all days for your grandiose visions. The prisoner Ravi is arriving tonight, and we have been instructed by a very FAMOUS AND IMPORTANT"—he glared at the gardener— "priest, who knows many MORE THINGS THAN YOU DO, Maali sahib. He has explained to us what we must do, and I do not THINK you are going to change this plan now. Focus, please, on making this area the best it can be. Masterji Dan has planned to use this for his TV show, and also he needs to shoot earlier shots and footage for his show. Surely, Maali sahib, this is big enough for you. Your setup, see? On the TV screen. Seen by Australians and Englishpeople as a model of what a good Indian ceremony looks like. So quit your daydreaming and get to work!"

Maali nodded. "I will do what I can do, sir, but do not be expecting the miracles and do not be blaming me when this unceremonious ugly place does not look like a va-va-voom Bollywood production." He threw up his hands in a faux Bollywood dance pose for extra flair. "I have no time and nothing to work with. Not even decent flowers."

Maali sighed and looked down, dismissing whatever the Butler's response would be. He had a perspective on the biological nature of things that others did not, you see. Care and feeding and water and sunlight helped plants grow. So did suggestion, if you were to come down to it, in humans. Now the seed of a more ambitious religious ceremony had been planted. One had only to voice a statement for it to take root. There were few people, in his opinion, who could ignore a stimulus; no more so than a plant can ignore the stimulus of fertilizer and sun. Maybe his barb would bear fruit before the evening. Maybe the Butler would come through with some exotic, high-end plants or decorations. In the meantime, his conscience was clear. Not his fault, was it now?

Maali took a deep drag of his locally produced, hand-rolled cigarette and crouched into a squat, pushing his knobby knees through the starched pants defiantly, to begin his work.

Back at the central Varanasi police station, the Panditji arrived in the late morning, but it was too late. Not that he knew anything about the previous visitors.

"Inspectorji," the Panditji said upon sitting down, immediately seeking to control the conversation. "A member of my respected, world-renowned yoga school has gone missing in Varanasi. I have heard he is in your prison as we speak. You must release him."

"Sri Panditji," the Inspectorji said, making a gesture of namaste, "it is unfortunate, and you are correct that we did apprehend a man who fits the description of a yogi earlier yesterday. You see, he was caught trespassing on someone's property."

"He must be released!" the Panditji said haughtily.

"Ah, that is not so simple," the Inspectorji said, shaking a finger in the air. He knew his jurisdiction well. Normally a man of the Panditji's stature was someone to kowtow to, but it was not every day that a bribe of this nature came in. Two bribes, if he played it right. "A concerned party has come to my attention, with a counter claim on your party member."

"What sort of concerned party? What sort of counter claim?" the Panditji said, his ire rising.

"Oh, that is not for you to be concerned about," the Inspectorji said, smiling.

"This will not stand!" the Panditji yelled, standing up. A lifetime of obsequious flattery did not prepare him well for this affront.

"Well now, Mr. Sir Panditji. Please, please, do not worry overmuch. Your party member is being treated very safely in our prison. He will be held just a few more days, as is in accordance with our laws. If we cannot prove his trespassing led to any direct thievery or malfeasance, he will be released. Surely, a man such as yourself understands patience. Hehe!" He giggled at his own clever joke. "After all what is the very big deal about a few days, anyway, in the grand scheme of things?" He held up his hands with a worldly air.

"Hmmphhh" was the Panditji's reply. "Surely, something can be done?"

"Nothing to be done, my good chap. Just wait a few minor days. He is in good hands. He will be released." The Inspectorji took a sip of his rapidly cooling tea.

That did it.

The Panditji took this as the final insult. To not even be offered tea? He rose and stormed out of the room. He could not recall being treated so poorly in a long time.

As the Panditji made his way across the tamped-down grassy field back to the waiting car, a tall, thin policeman came running out.

"Sir, sir!"

"What is it?" the Panditji snapped, holding the car door as he prepared to get in.

"Sir, that is, I can help with..." the policeman started, catching his breath.

"With what? How would you know what I need help with?" The Panditji eyed the policeman up and down distastefully. The man wore a shirt stained with oil and reeking of tobacco.

"With the prisoner, yes?"

"Go on."

"Well, I know where they are taking him."

"Taking him? Why should they be taking him anywhere? I thought he was supposed to be held for a few days in the jail."

"Sir, sir, please do not be upset. Just, if you could, you know..." The policeman looked down.

"What is your rank? Are you even capable of providing this information you are suggesting you have?"

"Sir, I graduated third honors in my class. Just, uh, provide the funding for myself and two others, and we shall ensure that you get your man. He is to, uh, leave the police station around 5pm today."

"What? That damn Inspectorji lied to me!" the Panditji barked. "Okay, you have a deal. You come with your colleagues. 4pm sharp today. To my guesthouse. No funny business, okay? Then we will reclaim the prisoner." The Panditji wordlessly got back in the car, watching the young, disheveled policeman run back inside. Nothing ever was lost, he thought, that could not be found again.

A sense of total ennui pervaded Ravi's entire being as he sat in his jail cell. He looked contemptuously at a deputy playing a game on his phone and giggling at text messages, maybe to a girlfriend. This existence, Ravi thought, had been so long, and he was exhausted from the constant circling of life. Nothing ever changed. Roads were built, then they were paved, then the rains came to wash them away. People decried the rains.

They cursed them. They said they would build differently next time. Stronger materials. Longer-lasting quality. More workers. Even so, Ravi thought, those roads always, always washed away again. Nature outlasted and outbid any impulse of man. As would he. As would the Panditji. He looked up as the Inspectorji approached to unlock his cell with a large metal key that hung from a ring.

"Come! You are to be transported," he said sternly.

Ravi shrugged, assuming the Panditji was coming for him, and went without a fight. He willingly climbed into a green police jeep, where he was handcuffed to restraints along the walls, and endured a bumpy ride with two young deputies on either side of him and the Inspectorji in the front. All the men wore the standard-issue olive green uniform with beret, and at least two sported the curling, luxurious mustache favored by men with authority in these parts.

The anxiety of what was about to come sent Jaya, dizzy, to her room.

"I'm okay," she reassured a worried Josh. "It's just all so much, and it's happening so fast." Despite herself, she lost it and started to cry. The constant fear and panic were beyond her capacity to handle. Knowing that they had no choice but to proceed with this ceremony and that she would see Ravi—all tonight—was more than she thought she could take.

"You've been awesome, Jaya. Finding Ravi. Escaping the Panditji when he tried to poison you. You've survived so much already. You can certainly handle this," Josh tried to reassure her.

As wonderful as it was to see Josh there, caring and kind, she wished desperately that they had met under some other, happier circumstances. No matter what happened, she would always associate Josh with the Panditji, and this crazy chapter in her life. That thought made her sadder, and she started crying harder, deep sobs. Josh held her helplessly. He fingered the book in his hands, the one that had caused them so much grief. It looked like any other ordinary hymn book. If only. Like her, he wished that they had met some other way. Now, he'd never know if he was drawn to her for the mystery of it all, or for her herself. He hoped whatever the reason, the outcome would be the same.

"Madam," the Butler said. Jaya looked up, her face tear-stained. "The ritual, they are ready. You are to come now. Master Dan has all the cameras set up."

"If you're sure, Jaya," Josh said, with love in his eyes. "Only if you're sure. You can stay back."

"It's okay, Josh. I have to do this. Mrs. Kumar is right. Butler, tell Dan and Nisha, we'll be right there." Newly determined, she got up, changed her clothes, wiped her face, and strolled out and into a waiting vehicle.

CHAPTER FIFTEEN

A Cleansing Fire

Dan's crew announced their presence at the Kala Ghat by blasting it with bright floodlights. As they arrived for the ceremony at dusk, Jaya noticed the place had been transformed. The stone platform down the steps was now ornately decorated and ready for a pooja, as it had probably not been in decades. Maali had indeed risen above the challenge. The cracked stones were shrouded in thick, brilliantly orange silks that gleamed when they caught the light. Strategically placed low-lying flowers in leafy planters covered particularly decrepit sections. Jaya spotted the elderly Pujari and Srikanth, the priest, already there preparing for the ritual.

"Places, everyone! Places!" Dan shouted. He was seated on his director's chair, with a megaphone in his hand, whipping up a whirlwind of action. "Jaya, Josh, you sit in the front of the fire please. Mrs. Kumar just next to them."

Josh and Jaya exchanged a look, silently rolling their eyes at Dan's controlling ways. Nevertheless, they went to their assigned places, joining the two holy men. In one hand, Jaya clutched the Panditji's diary—still wrapped in an old sari—to her chest and held Josh's hand with the other. Her nerves were jangled, perched as they were, metaphorically, on the edge of something evil, or at least unconventional. She'd never seen a Hindu ritual performed anywhere, except at a house or a temple. This untried approach filled Jaya with fear. Seated in the center of the stone platform, Srikanth and the Pujari were clothed in their crisp white Brahmin's dhotis, steadily building the ritual fire that would fuel tonight's ceremony.

At the embankment above the Kala Ghat, a police jeep came screeching to a stop. Inside the vehicle, Ravi recognized the ghat from so long ago, where it had all began with him and the Panditji. He would remember this place, always, even through the passage of time. "What mischief is this?" he asked with contempt. "But how do *you* know this place?" Ravi turned to the Inspectorji with inquisitive eyes.

The Inspectorji, ignoring him, wordlessly shimmied a handcuffed Ravi out of the vehicle. Greeted by the floodlights, Ravi winced and attempted to move his constrained hand to shield his eyes, but failed to move his hands very far. A video camera assaulted his vision, hovering just a few inches from his face.

"What's it like, Ravi, head disciple of Panditji Kaaju Maharaj, to be over seven hundred years old?" Dan threw out, shock-jock style, as Ravi was marched down to the ghat. "Do you care to comment, for our viewers?"

Though he was already taken aback by how much these people seemed to know about him and the Panditji, Ravi affected the calmest and most pleasant demeanor that he could and responded, "Surely, sir, you have me confused with someone else?" He looked into the camera, for added effect. *Remember, Ravi,* he said to himself calmly. *This person is a mortal. Stay calm. It does not matter. He'll be gone some day and you'll still be here.*

"*So*, today we are going to the one and only Kala Ghat of Varanasi," Dan said to the video camera. "No, you haven't heard of it, because its name has been banished for *all* eternity from the record of this ancient, holy city. Until tonight. The Kala Ghat. Mysterious. Some say an abomination. An impurity. We take a step into the dark. My crew and I defile ourselves. For the sake of our viewers. This man knows more. We learn more. Tonight. 11pm. Will we survive? Follow us and find out."

The cameras never left Ravi. There were two of them, held by assistants, capturing multiple angles. As Ravi made his way down toward the water, flanked by the Inspectorji's men, he saw the bright yellow flames of the live fire, and hitched with a start. Could it be, that these people knew about the moksha chakra ceremony? It had been so long ago. Could he and his darling Panditji survive being exposed like this? He searched his memory and could not think of any moment in his past lives where their secret had been discovered. After so many lives, Ravi had to admit he was unsure of how to solve this particular pickle. He was forced down, to sit on a cushioned pillow near the fire. The priests ignored him as they continued their preparations. The people around him would not make eye contact either, including, he saw now, Jaya. *Oh, of course. Of course, it was her.* He took a moment to admire her tenacity, then immediately replaced that emotion with uncut anger. How dare she be the one who exposed his secret. And what scheme was she up to with these video cameras and the priests? He stared dispassionately at the man next to her, admiring the contours of his face. A good-looking man, Ravi thought. But it didn't matter. Sooner or later, he and the Panditji would resolve this situation, and take their revenge. Of that, he was certain.

"Cut!" someone yelled. The filming stopped, momentarily, waiting for the next scene to be set up.

"Are we ready then?" Dan inquired of the priests.

"Yes, sir, yes, we are!" Srikanth looked earnest and determined. In his lap sat an open book of Hindu scripture. It took one of his hands and one knee to keep it propped open. One half of the book rested on the Pujari's lap next to him.

"Action!" Dan bellowed, indicating to his crew that the camera should point downwards to capture the fire and, of course, the Panditji's diary, which Jaya was holding onto tightly. Off to the side, the camera's light blinked red.

The Pujari began with the deep and low hum of the all-encompassing phrase denoting the beginning of the universe: "Ooooommmmmmm," he droned, and the rest joined him so that the full complement of voices covered a range of available sound.

Jaya took a deep breath to calm herself, realizing that in this moment, they were actually going to proceed with Srikanth's ritual of undoing the moksha chakra. Srikanth's clear, loud, nasal mantras reached straight to the heavens as he began. His dark eyes looked ahead, focused, his neck and back straight, while he recited the stanzas from memory. Speaking continuously with short pauses to catch his breath, his chanting was loud and confident; this was a man who fully believed he could return someone to their natural state. After all, he did a brisk business in his hometown doing only this sort of pooja. Had his reputation not spread? Did women not come with their newborns to him for this ceremony? He had never seen to this day any parent returning to him with a complaint. In fact they came to him over and over, begging for help, with entreating and trusting eyes. So Srikanth became accustomed to his power, and he radiated a sense of purpose on this night.

Seated in his director's chair, Dan Katt was the omniscient one, capturing the expressions and the sounds of each participant.

Mrs. Kumar's elegant face wore a bemused expression. *It does not matter*, she thought, *if this Srikanth is not successful. So what? Many other holy men have held out their powers and overpromised. Still, I must do my part here, to protect Maalpur, and Jaya.* She concentrated her actions on being a very dutiful, very prompt helper for the priests. Perfectionism was an easy, knee-jerk reaction. As the priests performed the ritual, depositing offerings of rice, then flowers, then oil into the fire to build its direct connection to the universe, it was Mrs. Kumar who sat at attention. Each time the priest turned and motioned for her to bring him something from the pile of pre-prepared ceremonial goods, she would reach over, grab it in her cupped hands, and turn, as precisely and quickly as she could, creating as little torque as possible, an efficient human supply chain from supply pile to fire to air.

Ravi, being tonight's main villain and star, held Dan's focus repeatedly. Dan could see him staring down Srikanth, looking at him with antagonism.

I don't recognize these priests, Ravi fumed to himself. *What are they doing, anyway? This is not the moksha chakra ceremony. I don't understand why these people wouldn't want to have more power like I and the Panditji have, if they could.* Srikanth's voice was, to Ravi's ears, crudely braying in a rural accent the beautiful, sophisticated Sanskrit words. Shrugging at the futility of his anger, and accepting his situation in the Hindu way as a temporal moment that would pass, like being too hot or too cold, Ravi stared straight ahead and tried to clear his mind.

Jaya, the heroine, was where Dan's video camera panned to now. It showed her eyes gazing forward, not focusing on anything. What was she thinking?

I owe it to Josh and Mrs. Kumar and the Pujari and especially Dan to try to keep an open mind, and let Srikanth finish his ceremony tonight. Listen, if this fails, we'll have at least tried. But if it does fail, then I'm going to need to figure out what happens next, build a new project plan for my life. She could envision what might happen after this was over, right through the warped, smoky air. Ravi would be released and returned to the ashram to spend his time with the Panditji. She and Josh would make a hasty exit from India before any authorities could find them, and before they could get into further trouble with the Panditji and Ravi.

Drifting, her mind flashed to more banal things, like gifts. She had committed to bringing so many things back to her friends in New York. Incense. Pillow covers with camels on them. Real Assam tea. At best, she'd be buying overpriced knickknacks at the airport. *Focus, Jaya,* she thought to herself. Then the group chant brought her back.

In unison, the group was encouraged to chant the word "Swaahaa," drawing out the vowels, every time Srikanth finished a section of the ceremony. When he did this, he offered something to the fire: rice, flowers, oil. The fire absorbed the new liquids and roared up, just as their voices crescendoed in support. It was a hypnotic rhythm.

And let's see what Josh, our erstwhile hero, is doing, Dan Katt thought, swinging the camera over. He could see that Josh's face was one of concentration and awe.

I should listen carefully, Josh thought, *since I'm one of the few here who understands these Sanskrit words and texts.* His mind jumped about at the words he was hearing and the linguistic connections between this and his work. For a moment, he forgot his position and recent history as the protector of a woman tormented by the Panditji's secret, and he allowed his mind to run ferociously and venture into the possibilities and the unknowns, testing and circling, researching every potential outcome of this new, lived, real-life experience. No books this time, and no old texts. This was real and now and here in front of him; he was probably witnessing a thousand-year-old ceremony, handed down through generations. The top of his neck tingled slightly. It was hard to reconcile that he, a scholar who read books left by others, could be experiencing this warp in time himself.

Through all this, Dan also kept tabs on his fan base, many of whom were live-streaming this. A shock jolted happily through him as he watched the number of followers and viewers tick up, and emoji icons fill his screen. The thrill of connecting to an audience could keep him going forever. Dan's fan base—an un-likely-to-meet-in-real-life, bimodal distribution of preteen girls with crushes on his cute but approachable style, and rough-and-ready law enforcement aficionados—was ready for what he had to drop.

Srikanth's ceremony—its words and its fire and its offer-ings—blended together and took on momentum that swirled toward the heavens. And then, the gods who watch over us all deigned to look down to the earth to see this set of people and their priest's entreaties, and responded. Ravi's lost memories came flooding back to him, unbidden. Varanasi, Dan's house, being found, going to jail. Before this, meeting Jaya, realizing how much she knew, attempting to silence her. The fire swayed and dwindled with a rough gust of wind, then it roared back to life, twice as high as before. Ravi jerked slightly, and Dan's camera caught his movement, bringing the lens in closer for a tighter shot.

Ravi remembered moments much earlier, before this life, before Jaya and his life with the Panditji, his loving embraces, and the adoring global students. He remembered the superhu-man feeling in his supple body and his clear mind during yoga practice. His parents, whose house he had left to join the Pan-ditji. The feeling of love and gratitude when he looked upon the Panditji at any time.

Ravi felt his body disconnect, flipping over and over, while his mind lost its tightness. He slipped into a haze.

Dan's camera caught him in his zombie-like state.

Ravi saw himself and the Panditji, younger and chubbier, older and thinner, in different times, with different people dressed in different clothing. He saw the ashram full of men, with assistants waving handheld fans in the summer heat, in a world without electricity.

Memories of the Kala Ghat came, this place he was sitting on now, screaming, insisting to be heard, straight into the very front of his mind. He remembered the ceremony that had started it all, on a night with a new moon just like tonight. Back then it had been something he had desperately wanted to do. He had been an arrogant, good-looking twentysomething, in love with the Panditji, so besotted he could hardly see straight. To be with the Panditji, to prolong his time with him, he would have done anything, and so he eagerly awaited his own death at the Panditji's hands. The stabbing pain lasted much longer than he imagined it should have, and the wet feeling of blood saturating his clothes was followed by a gradual, dull exhaustion that overwhelmed his mortal body as the blood drained from it. When I died, I was excited beyond words. *There was so much hope. What a life I have lived, so much luxury and sweetness and power, all because of the Panditji*, he thought, as the last bits of his consciousness slipped away.

Ravi's memories came to an end, and all he could perceive was blackness. His body lost its rigor and slumped downwards, despite the Inspectorji's men holding him on either side.

Dan rose in his seat to get a better camera angle on Ravi's form.

"Wake him up!" the Pujari said urgently to the policemen guarding Ravi. "He must be awake for this ceremony to work."

Quick, short slaps were delivered to his face, and Ravi groggily came to. His eyes looked glazed. He had to be propped up as he slipped a few times sideways.

Dan, international fame-seeker, thanked the gods for his luck. How fortuitous it had been to meet Jaya and Josh a few weeks ago. This was the first true, unembellished case of the supernatural he'd ever seen. It was a drug, he realized, the real thing. Adrenalin filled him, and he hoped beyond hope that the ceremony had worked. He brought the lens in even tighter, so that he could see every movement of Ravi's eyes.

Ravi, now not-Ravi, sat upright, blank, awake, and confused. He felt hollow, like an empty box. His ears heard sounds from a distance, as if he were stuffed inside a water tank. They were talking about him, he could tell. He did not know why. Who were these people? He did not recognize any of them. Why was he here, away from his university? He needed to get back to prepare for his tests for his economics degree. The tests determined his future, which, if all went well, would be in the civil service. He had to get up, keep moving. But when he tried to stand, he found there were policemen keeping him in place, and they tightened their hands on his shoulder, which he hadn't noticed were gripping him until now.

"Look!" Jaya exclaimed. "Could the ceremony have worked?"

Dan flashed a thumbs-up sign, to indicate he agreed.

Josh threw his arm around her and yelped.

Mrs. Kumar gave a quick gasp of relief.

Yes, you see, a man whom everyone perceived to be Ravi was sitting there. Inside, he was now restored to whom he should have been all along from this birth, before Ravi, the Panditji's Ravi, had so rudely taken over his life. This is not-Ravi, a twenty-one-year-old student from the area near Varanasi, named Vishal. In fact, the ritual, the one that Srikanth had brought from the countryside, the one that was used for other purposes entirely? That one. It had worked. Not-Ravi now sat disoriented, amongst the urgency of Srikanth's attestations.

Srikanth, insisting on completing the ceremony, continued to chant single-mindedly, with assistance from Mrs. Kumar and the Pujari, who were both watching Ravi carefully and curiously.

Suddenly, a bar of glaring white lights appeared, overpowering Dan's camera lighting. Everyone turned to look at the headlights cresting over the hill. Car doors were heard opening and closing, and loud noises as well.

"Please! Pay attention!" the Pujari said in vain.

"Get whatever is up there, will you? I'll stay on the ceremony," Dan shouted to a secondary camera crew. *Glad I got that local auxiliary crew, tonight,* Dan thought. One could never be too prepared.

"Hey!" Josh shouted. "Something, or someone, is coming."

Jaya's stomach sank. *I guess this is it,* she thought, *the moment this fails and I go back to my old life.*

"Don't worry, Jaya. It's just tourists, that's all," Josh said.

"At *this* hour?" Jaya asked, doubtfully.

CHAPTER SIXTEEN

The Wheel of Life

"No, oh no!" Jaya yelled, putting her hands over her face. The person she had hoped never to see again had arrived. The Panditji, flanked by two police officers, was walking with agility down the adorned stone steps of the Kala Ghat.

"You!" the Panditji hissed, upon seeing Jaya. "And Ravi! There you are, my love." His searching face found his missing partner's form. "So, Jaya, I see you have a little ceremony going, is it now? Whatever mischief you're getting into, I think we'll soon take care of it."

"Go ahead and try us!" Jaya said, without thinking of the consequences. Srikanth wasn't finished yet, and she felt she needed to give him the space to finish what he had started to make sure it had *really* worked. Jaya felt Josh grab her arm to distance her away from the Panditji.

The Panditji, with his yogic flexibility, quickly planted himself on the ground next to them. His face heaved with anger. Jaya spontaneously shivered, frightened by the raw look of hatred in his eyes and the painful memories that his presence brought back.

"I'm so glad you have the fire going, Jaya. This will make your moksha chakra ceremony so much easier. You remember? The one I told you about," the Panditji said, chillingly. Before Jaya could even contemplate what to say, he wrenched Jaya from Josh's grip, twisting her arm under her in a way that hurt. As she screamed, she had no choice but to follow the Panditji. At the same time, Josh reached out and tried to pull her back, but failing, he fell face first onto the stone floor, banging his nose.

"Ravi!" the Panditji yelled.

There was no response whatsoever from not-Ravi.

The Panditji screamed again. "Ravi! Can you hear me?"

And again, there was no response.

"Won't work!" Jaya gasped through the pain, directing her words at the Panditji. "Your Ravi's gone. Thanks to our friends, we've reversed the moksha chakra!" Tears beaded in Jaya's eyes in relief, as she realized that what she had just said was for real. The ceremony, it had to have actually worked. The Panditji's evil had been reversed.

"Hurry, Srikanth," Dan yelled, "you have to finish this up!" Abandoning his camera and sensing trouble, Dan's inner action-hero engaged, and he motioned to his assistants to carry on filming while he took care of things. He jumped out of his chair, pulling a gleaming silver-colored pistol from the back of his pants and aiming it in the direction of the Panditji and the fire. Mrs. Kumar, terrified by the sight of a weapon, awkwardly stood and ran from the fire, sobbing, tradition and duty be damned. The Pujari and Srikanth kept chanting.

"Ravi," the Panditji said urgently, dragging Jaya across the stone floor as he moved toward his lover. "Answer me, my love."

"Why am I here? Who are you?" shouted not-Ravi, looking at the Panditji with confusion in his eyes. "I don't know who this Ravi is. I am Vishal. There's been some big mistake. I'm a student, going to take my college exams. I don't know Ravi. Surely, you can please let me go." And then turning inward he began to pray, "Oh Hanuman, please, now, please take me away."

"Please! My love!" the Panditji bellowed. "Please Ravi." He reached out with one hand to try to touch his beloved Ravi, but in that moment, Ravi flinched. Then the Panditji knew. Ravi was lost to him. Possibly forever.

"Aarrrhghhhththghghgh!" Unable to handle the anguish, the Panditji screamed into the sky at no one in particular.

While he was distracted, Jaya, realizing she still held the Panditji's diary in her hands, dropped it surreptitiously onto the floor in front of her feet. If she survived this, she would need this documentation. Otherwise, who would even believe her crazy story?

"He's gone, Panditji. He's gone forever. You'll never get him back," Jaya said, defiantly.

The Panditji's eyes darkened, and he turned toward her. He pulled out a dagger from his pants pocket. Jaya gasped when she saw it. She felt the tip of the dagger's blade pushing into her abdomen, drawing blood. She shut her eyes and joined the Panditji in his screams.

"Hey! Stop it!" Josh said, helplessly.

"Yes! Yes, I will stop this, this abomination of a ceremony!" the Panditji shouted at Josh. Without warning, the Panditji pulled the dagger out of Jaya so that he could casually knife a still-chanting Srikanth in the neck. The Panditji hardly even blinked. Srikanth gasped, eyes widening, blood flowing all over the place, down his cotton shirt and mixing with the dirt into a sticky mess. Clutching his throat, he fell over as the words sputtered and then stopped coming out of his mouth. In the background, Mrs. Kumar let out a low, agonizing moan, and fainted straight away.

The older Pujari, sitting next to the now deposed Srikanth, blanched and, while still reciting a Hindu prayer, got up to run, tripping over his dhoti as he scrambled away from the source of the violence. The ritual to undo the moksha chakra, whatever might be left of it, had come to an end with Srikanth's death.

Josh, vomiting at the sight of the dead priest, valiantly stayed put near the fire, pulling himself up next to Jaya and watching for an opportunity to rescue them both.

For a long minute, there was silence. And then, the Panditji began to chant.

"It can't be," the Pujari, shaken. He was comforting a now conscious Mrs. Kumar a safe distance from the ritual fire. "Those words that this Panditji are chanting. It is the original. The moksha chakra. The one I told you about from so long ago. Oh, Hai Bhagvan. What evil has befallen this place."

Mrs. Kumar shuddered, covering her face with her hands.

Dan, meanwhile, was creeping in the shadows, getting closer to the fire and the Panditji, gun outstretched in his hand. He whispered breathlessly into his headset to his crew, "Ladies, lads, you better not lose this footage."

The Panditji chanted the moksha chakra that he knew by heart. It was hard and humorless, lacking the melody of the earlier ritual. As he intoned the words, the fire, which had waned slightly, came roaring back. The air became smokier and dirtier, and a foul odor took over.

You've got to do something, Jaya thought to herself as the Panditji chanted. *That poor priest, he died because of me. Think, Jaya.* She could feel his frustration and anger, and helplessness. Ignoring the screeching pain in her abdomen, she shifted her foot closer to the diary.

"Hey, Panditji! Was this what you were looking for?" she gasped, looking down.

It was enough to distract him. He stopped chanting.

"Oh! Don't you dare!" the Panditji warned when he saw the diary at her feet. "This is my property, my history. Who are you to try to take it from me!"

"It's my history, too!" Jaya shouted. So saying, she shot her foot out and kicked the diary—the one that had caused so much trouble, documented so much evil—hard, so that it spun, skipped over a crack in the stones, and hopped straight into the fire pit. The gods accepted this new offering heartily, and the diary's ancient pages, dried with age, sparked and crinkled, losing all form and function, within a matter of a few moments.

Enraged, the Panditji reached over to her, brandishing his dagger.

That was when a gunshot rang out. Dan, aiming from above, hit the Panditji directly in the heart.

As thunder crackled through the clouds, portending a true storm, the Panditji's form shook as he chanted. Bathed in the firelight, his face swayed, lit up in tones of yellow and purple. His white kurta was stained red. Jaya felt the knife lose its pressure, as the Panditji fumbled with his grip. Blindly, Jaya grabbed the knife's handle and flipped it away from herself, turning the blade on her tormentor.

"Die again, why don't you," she said in a low, husky voice. Closing her eyes, she took a deep breath and plunged the knife into the Panditji's hard stomach, ignoring her squeamishness as she felt the resistance that the Panditji's impeccable musculature put up.

Blood now flowed from the Panditji's body. Lifting his head as high as he could, he tried to speak.

"...Can't die... I will... come back... ha..." He twisted his face into a half-grimace, half-smile. "You ca-can't kill me."

Then his head dropped suddenly, his forehead hitting the Kala Ghat's platform with a thud. There was total silence. The Panditji's mouth hissed, expelling his last breath, laughing at his own in-joke. His face stayed frozen in place, as the rest of his body settled and then hardened.

No one spoke. Dan aimed his pistol and shot the body twice more for good measure. Each time the body jerked slightly from the impact.

A sense of lightness glided straight through Jaya's mind. The fear that had gripped her was gone. Her body was free. Her mind as well. She turned and clutched Josh, who was right there, and he hugged her as tight as he possibly could, patted her hair, and said sweet things to her. Tears flowed out of her from relief.

Up above the Kala Ghat, the Inspectorji's men had handcuffed their two turncoat colleagues and were putting them in the police jeep. At their superior's nod, they came running towards the inert body of the Panditji and started to document the scene in what was routine police procedure. They pulled out their phones and took video and photos, circling around to get all angles. Next to them, Dan's crew continued to get footage for the show.

The Inspectorji extracted a small pad of paper from his front pocket and then a pen. He wrote slowly, while reading his notations out loud so that his men could capture it on their video log.

"One male. Perpetrator. Deceased. Stab wound and gunshot wound to flank. Gunshot wounds to both legs. Age approchimately forty to fifty. Second male. Victim. Deceased. Stab wound to neck. Age approchimately thirty. One female. Victim acting in self-defense. Sustained stab wound to stomach. Alive. Age approchimately thirty years. Witnesses present confirm as such."

As the Inspectorji finished his dictation, fat rain drops came tumbling with accelerating speed out of the thundering sky. In shock, Jaya stayed in Josh's arms, paying no attention to the rain that soaked her hair and washed the blood from her body.

"He's gone. He's gone. He's gone," she kept mumbling to herself, as she rocked herself back and forth. "He's gone. He's gone. He's gone."

Josh threw a police blanket over her, hugging her over it and trying to keep her warm. "Don't worry now, Jaya. You were so brave. Without you, we'd never have gotten rid of him." She tilted her head into his neck, allowing the tears and the sweet release of them to come over her. Everyone moved around them, as they sat. An ambulance pulled up, and medical workers came to examine Jaya.

The commotion was broken by Dan Katt.

"What a psychopath," he said, staring at the Panditji's body. "Here, chaps, help me throw this jerk into the fire. Let's give him a proper burial, shall we?"

The surviving holy man, the Pujari, shook his head and threw up his hands as he saw what they were about to do. "No! Please do not defile this already-bad place any more," he pleaded. But he was ignored.

Dan and Josh and the policemen all swarmed the Panditji's body, lifting it unevenly by the arms and legs. The torso sagged as they placed it into the rain-dampened ceremonial fire. The body lay unevenly there amongst the wooden sticks and the remaining pieces of the diary, arms and legs hanging outside the pit. Dan's cameras caught the black kohl bleeding from the Panditji's half-closed eyes and running down his cheeks.

"He'll come back, you know," Jaya said to the group. "We got rid of him for now. His soul can still come back to find me."

"Yes, but you freed me, apparently," Vishal said shyly.

"And you gave me one hell of a story, love!" Dan whooped.

"And not to mention, you exposed a serial killer," Josh said, admiringly.

"Now, Jaya," Mrs. Kumar said. "You must trust me on this. I've seen the Panditji now twice, in this life. He is truly evil. You've done a very brave thing. The town of Maalpur thanks you, and I know your Daadi Ma and your family, they will be very very proud of you, too."

Jaya smiled. She could hope that for now, she might remain free of the Panditji, at least for the rest of her natural life. For now, that was enough.

The Maalpur Yoga Ashram

Seven months later, the Pandit Kaaju Maharaj (PKM) Ashram reopened for international visitors as the rebranded Maalpur Yoga Ashram (MYA). Jaya, with some help from her mother's friend who worked at a New Jersey savings bank, had applied for and successfully received a loan to reinvest in the ashram, and to reclaim her father's ancestral lands. With the differential in exchange rates, the loan in US dollars went a long way.

Jaya, ever the project manager, approached her new career as a yoga ashram owner with gusto, recruiting yoga teachers, advertising for students, and managing expenses tightly. The MYA radiated with a revamped temple, updated living quarters, and, thanks to positive reviews started by Barb and Angie, a small and growing stream of students from India, South Korea, Japan, Australia, France, Israel, and the US. For the first time in her life, Jaya had a purpose. Her purpose was to enable whatever it was that the people who visited her ashram needed: a vacation, a rest, a spiritual quest. She found that supplying her guests with those experiences was itself a full-time job.

Jaya also invested in a good contractor to seal off the rooms near the temple where she had found the Panditji's book and nearly lost her life. Never again would any nefarious deeds be done there.

Josh's translation of the Panditji's diary, and the underlying books that had driven Jaya on her quest, had been the subject of much debate. At first, Daadi Ma and Mrs. Kumar, now in regular communication on video chat, were of the opinion that the translation must be donated to the government of India to be housed in a collection of historical mysteries in the National Museum in Delhi. But ultimately, in consultation with the Pujari, they decided that, given that they were all mortal and the Panditji was not, the information must be housed somewhere sufficiently protected, where only the family and the descendants of the family might be able to find it, and where future Panditjis, when they came seeking, could be easily exposed.

This was when Josh came up with the idea of filming an archival documentary and making it publicly available. It would chronicle all of the Panditji's exploits, his images throughout the years, and append interviews with locals including Mrs.

Kumar. The project was something Josh could uniquely help with, and he reasoned that transparency was the only way to protect themselves against someone as devious as the Panditji, especially since they had to take into account what future residents of the ashram might do after they were long dead.

Josh's documentary was, of course, underwritten, produced, directed, and reenacted by Dan Katt and his muse, Nisha. The movie, dedicated to the valiant priest Srikanth, became an instant hit, a cult favorite that would take on a life of its own. Dan became a bona fide A-list star. Nisha got her first big acting role. Josh was promoted to editor of a larger journal in New York. And Jaya's ashram became the subject of intense interest. Each handled their newfound fame rather well.

The yoga world was, of course, shocked to watch Dan's documentary, and even more horrified to find that a yogi mystic whom they regarded as one of their own was a modern-day murderer who had bastardized the rules of life to live forever. They were used to stories of yogis with too much power doing the wrong things, but this was something singularly wicked.

Many of the Panditji's former students felt contrite at what they had unwittingly perpetuated, and while they were thankful for what they had learned, they sought a new sort of refuge, one that helped them to atone for the unwitting sins they might have funded or supported in the past. This atonement they found in Jaya's new ashram.

Amid all this, Jaya had decided to take a one-year break from Josh. The old Jaya, back in New York, would not have done this. She would have gone through her list of ex-boyfriends, willing to consider men once or twice, or three times, no matter their behavior. But, she was stronger now, and more willing to challenge the universe to meet her higher expectations. And, she had the confidence to wait for what might unfold, and the wherewithal to choose when to respond. As she had explained to Josh, they had been thrown together as travelers and seekers, through circumstances that were dangerous and unusual. It remained to be seen if, without the heightened drama, as ordinary people, they would still have what it took to sustain a longer-term relationship. Though she missed him terribly already, this was the right thing to do. For now.

And still, the threat of the Panditji's return circled. At some point in the future, a reconstituted Panditji would return to this earth, and rebuild. This eventuality was never far from her mind. As she understood now, his path to power was rooted in individual suffering. Denial of basic needs for sleep, for food, for sex, it is believed, would remove extraneous variables, concentrate energies, and stimulate the universe to work in our favor. And so, she imagined the Panditji was now on a strict regimen of fasting and yoga, doing what came as a natural crutch to people in ancient times seeking to restore an imbalance. Each day, she could see it. The Panditji awakening, eating a sparse breakfast of vegetables and grains, and then assembling himself under a leafy tree in the courtyard. She sees him now, and he is fashioning his limbs into a tree pose: standing on one leg, the other leg bent, foot tucked into knee, his arms bent in a prayer position, and his hands held to his forehead, his eyes closed, his back completely straight. When the day's end comes, a large brass bell is struck, and the Panditji takes some time to respond. You see, his consciousness may as well have been fifty feet underwater, and the gong sounds from a distance, requiring him to swim back from a place of deep retreat into the present. Sound returns, then touch, then smell, then sight, and then finally when the fast is broken, taste. And when he does eat, there is intense pain as the stomach juices in his body hungrily swirl to devour what little food he ingests.

One morning, as Jaya drank her morning cup of coffee on a veranda at the ashram, a man came through the gates. He was dressed as a beggar, in saffron robes. A sadhu. A wise man. She smiled at him kindly and gave him oatmeal from the kitchen and a cup of hot tea. He refused to sit on the chairs, so she arranged a mat for him on the marble floor, where he sat quietly, eating. Then, a sense of calm overtook her whole being as she watched this man feel comforted by the food and shelter she gave him.

This was her land, and the land of her forefathers. It had been stolen from them, for a while, through the negligence of time and gaps in paternity. Now, it was returned back to her. Along the way, she had experienced the effects of great evil, one that had been born and had bred itself in this very same place, and through the efforts of her and her friends, they had extinguished that evil for one lifetime.

She also had seen the inner workings of centuries of tradition. She had seen how apostasy unfolded and continued through the Kala Ghat. And it was a triumph to her that somehow, through all of this, she had made her way through and survived. What she felt now was the dawning of a sense of wisdom that came from having seen the natural order of things being upset. And that meant, unfortunately, that the prospect of returning to a life in New York, to a flat with a roommate, to another project management job, was somewhat unthinkable. She wasn't the same person.

Now, her new life as the owner of a yoga ashram in the middle of India in a small town was not some perfect paradise either. There were daily struggles, such as keeping house workers on staff, electricity and water shortages, currency fluctuations, and the ongoing nightmare of shipping packages to and from the United States. It was as if she had traded one set of life's complications for another set. But she chose to accept it, just as she must accept that the Panditji would never be completely gone. When one removes their attachments in life, she thought, even to things so basic as safety, to things so basic as order, one could live in a state of acceptance. Acceptance, as Jaya knew, is the first step in the ability to see the truth. And, when you see the truth, free of delusions, after all the illusions, there is lasting wisdom.

Namaste.

Acknowledgements

This book would not have been possible without the guidance and support of fellow writers and friends. I want to thank my parents, Om and Shuby Dewan, my sister, Sheri Dewan, and friends, Laura Shafferman and Caroline O'Connor for their encouragement and support of my writing. I want to thank my editor, Eldes Tran, who edited the book with a ferocity and precision I respect and admire, and Matina Korologos Velez, whose brilliant cover design captured the mystery of a woman lost and then finding herself. Most of all, I want to thank my husband Matt Doty, for being my first reader, and daughter Kavi Dewan Doty, who was born in the process of editing this novel. To anyone who says it's not possible to be a mom and an author, this novel is for you.

About the Author

Priya Doty is an author, wife, mom, and tech marketing executive based in Brooklyn, New York. She holds a liberal arts degree in economics from Northwestern University, and an MBA from MIT Sloan. She has traveled to over 30 countries, grew up in Saudi Arabia, and was part of the cast of the Academy-Award winning short film, *God of Love*. *Finding Warrior Pose* is her first novel.

Made in the USA
Middletown, DE
13 May 2022

65718228R00172